Seven White Gates

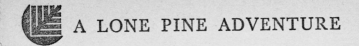

A LONE PINE ADVENTURE

Seven
White Gates

MALCOLM SAVILLE

Collins
LONDON AND GLASGOW

First published in this edition 1971

ISBN 0 00 160222 5

PRINTED AND MADE IN GREAT BRITAIN BY
WM. COLLINS SONS AND CO. LTD.
LONDON AND GLASGOW

Contents

Foreword

IN the county of Shropshire, not very far from the
borders of Wales, there stretches for five miles a gaunt,
rugged range called Stiperstones. This little-known mountain is crowned by a mysterious ridge known as the Devil's
Chair, which is said to be one of the oldest parts of England
—older by far even than the ice age.

It is in this country—a fragment of England rich in
folklore and legend—that this story is set. Except for the
two villages through which Peter rode on the first day
of the Easter holidays, you will not find any other of the
places mentioned on a map. They do not exist. There is
no village called Barton Beach, no valley called Black
Dingle and no farm—so far as I know—with seven white
gates. All the people you will read about are imaginary
and have no reference to any living person.

But if you ever discover the Stiperstones for yourself
you will find that the Devil's chair is there. I promise
you that.

M. S.

David Morton drew this Map of SEVEN GATES and the Dingle and the Cable Railway at H.Q.2 the morning after the Reunion Feast.

Signpost

Cottages   White Door   Barns

6th Gate

3rd Gate

5th Gate

1st. Gate

2nd Gate

4th Gate

TRACK TO FARM FIELDS

BARTON BEACH

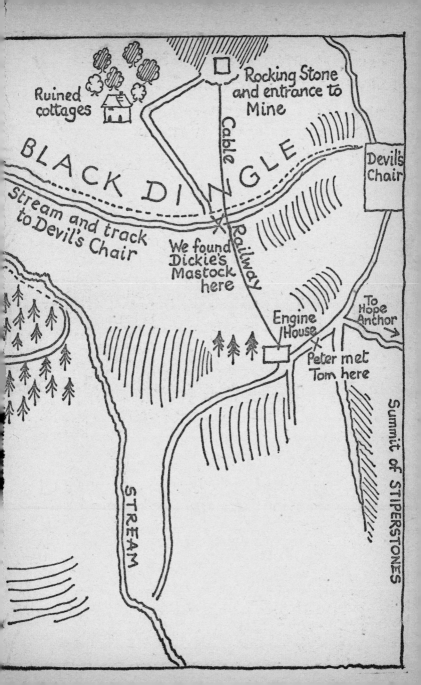

1. *Lone Pine Summons*

FOR AS LONG as she had been a boarder at the Castle School Peter had felt peculiar on the last day of term.

It had always been the same, and now that she was fifteen and would be taking School Certificate in the summer, she felt just as excited and sick as she had at the end of that long first term when she was only ten and had cried into her pillow: "*Tomorrow* I shall really go home. *Tomorrow* I shall see Daddy. *Tomorrow* I shall go up the valley again to lovely Hatchholt."

Now, at breakfast-time on breaking-up morning before the Easter Holidays, she looked round the crowded tables and wondered how it was that all the other laughing, chattering girls were able to produce normal appetites on such an exciting day. She turned to the girl on her left.

"You can have my fish-cake, Margaret. I'm not hungry and I suppose you are—as usual!"

"I should just think I am! What's the matter, Peter?"

"Nothing. I only want my tea, that's all."

"Well, you look a bit green . . . But you'd better not report to Matron in case you've got something catching, and they keep us all from going home."

Peter sat back and crumbled her bread. Her throat felt a little tight, and she was conscious of the thumping of her heart as she wondered whether all these other girls with whom she had spent most of her life loved their homes as much as she did. And Peter was well aware that she had an unusual home. There were only three other girls at the Castle who, like herself, had no mother, and that made a difference, of course. But nobody else lived in a tiny, isolated cottage at the top of a lonely valley in the Shropshire hills, with a dear old Daddy who was in charge of one of the reservoirs which supplied the Midland cities with water. Only Joanna, at the end of the next table, had a pony, and although Peter had never seen it, she was sure that it was a most expensive, purebred animal, and not at all like her precious, sure-footed mountain pony, Sally.

Peter had never found anyone who knew as much about the country as she did; nobody who loved birds and wild things in the same way; nobody who had climbed the hills and picked bilberries higher than the streams began, and nobody who would steal out with her at night to watch the stars swing across the blue-black sky.

All this did not mean that Peter was not happy at school —she was. She had many friends, but no one special friend, and not until the Mortons had come to Witchend last summer had she ever preferred anyone else's company to her own. Now, of course, after their amazing adventure together, they would always be very special friends, and she was longing to meet them all again tomorrow. She was just wondering whether there would be a letter from David this morning when the headmistress rose from her place and reduced one hundred and sixty girls and a large staff to silence. She gave out a few notices, and then, after the grace, the girls filed out of hall to go to their own houses.

In Pollards, the morning letters were always put out on the mantelpiece in the hall, and as Peter was first in, she had to rummage through quite a big pile before she found two for her. The first was unmistakably from her father, and she was surprised he had found it necessary to send her a second letter this week, for she had had one the day before. She wondered what he had forgotten to tell her, but examined the other envelope first.

The address on this was not nearly as legible. The writer had written Peter first, and then crossed it out and substituted "Petronella Sterling, Pollards House, Castle School, Shrewsbury." On the back of the envelope was a crude drawing of a pine tree and a printed message written in copying ink which read: "WE'RE HOME BOTH OF

US TWO." Peter laughed. Just like the twins to have the
last word!

Half-way along the corridor to the house room was
a window with a deep seat. Peter hurried there now with
her two letters, swung her legs up and opened her father's
envelope.

"MY DEAR PETRONELLA," she read hurriedly, "I have
some surprising news for you which will, I fear, necessitate
some change in our immediate plans. No sooner had Ward,
the postman, collected my letter to you last Monday than
the telephone rang. You will remember how much I dislike
this instrument, and indeed, since its installation after the
events of last summer, I have yet to receive anything but
disquieting or unexpected news from it. This occasion was
no exception . . ."

Peter's eyes flew down the page in the hope of finding
the real news before she realized that she would have to
go back to the beginning to get the full story. Mr. Sterling
could never be hurried. She sighed and went back to the
top of the page.

". . . This occasion was no exception. I was told that
I was to proceed to the offices of the Water Company in
Birmingham on Thursday next, and that I must be
available for consultation for some days in that most
detestable city. You will realize, my dear Petronella, that
I have no choice in this matter, and it will therefore be
impossible for you to come to Hatchholt on that day. I
cannot permit you to stay here alone in the empty house,
and I have therefore telegraphed to—and received confirmation from—your uncle and aunt at their farm called
Seven Gates at Barton Beach. I have asked them to
accommodate you until we can both return to Hatchholt
together. I do not know how long I shall be away, but I
suggest that you send your trunk to Onnybrook ready for
transport here, and that you should cycle to Barton Beach
on Thursday, taking what you need in your haversack.

"Yesterday I paid one of my rare visits to Witchend to

see your young friends. All are very well, and I found the twins in exceptionally good form. My sight is not what it was, but it would seem to me that they are even more alike than they were last summer, and that their strange aptitude for simultaneous conversation and for finishing each other's thoughts and sentences has strengthened rather than diminished. Mrs. Morton was so kind as to suggest that you go to them until I return, and although I know that you would welcome this, I prefer that you should go to Seven Gates.

"You will hardly remember your Uncle Micah and have never met your Aunt Caroline. I do not know her well, but you will recall that she has often invited you and it is discourteous to continue to refuse such hospitality. You may find your uncle a little strange and life somewhat different on a large farm, but I am sure that you will do all you can to help your aunt, who will give you a warm welcome.

"Your friend David seems to have grown also. He is a fine lad—always courteous and ready to listen to his elders . . ." Peter grinned ruefully at this observation. "He is coming over to Hatchholt tomorrow for your pony. Now that you have taught him to ride, I am sure Sally will be safe with him.

"You know, my dear Petronella, how much I dislike these upsets, but you will please me by making the best of this matter and doing all you can to help your uncle and aunt. I hope also that I shall receive a rather more satisfactory report of your progress at school this term.

"As soon as I know the date of my return I will write or telegraph you again.

"With love from your affectionate father,

"JASPER STERLING.

"P.S.—I have written to your headmistress by this post."

Through a mist of unshed tears Peter realized that the other girls were crowding past her down the corridor as they ran to get ready for "reading over" in the school hall. All very well for them to laugh! Their holidays were not spoiled. All her plans were ruined! Now she would not see her father next day, nor Sally, nor David, nor the twins, nor Tom, and she would not be there to open the Lone Pine Camp after its winter rest.

Now Dad was telling her to go off by herself to a place she had forgotten, to see an aunt she had never met and an old uncle with a beard like a prophet in the Old Testament, and of whom she felt half afraid.

Margaret's cheerful voice broke into her gloomy thoughts.

"What *is* up, Peter? You are feeble this morning, and you can't sit there glooming all the day. We're late for Hall already . . ." she paused a moment and then added quietly: "Bad news, Peter? . . . Sorry if I'm butting in . . ."

Peter jumped down, gulped and sniffed, and then slipped her arm through her friend's.

"Thanks, Margaret," she said. "I'm all right really. It's just that I can't go straight home tomorrow, but have got to go to some relations I don't know till Daddy comes back."

They just managed to get into Hall before the head took her place in the centre of the platform and started to read over the form order. During the applause and general excitement, Peter realized that she had not yet opened the other letter. She had pushed them both into the front of her tunic and she felt now for their reassuring crackle. They seemed to have slipped in her haste, and she was fumbling in a panicky way for them when Margaret nudged her violently and hissed . . . "It's you, you silly ass . . . *Peter!* She's calling you . . . *Go up and get it!*"

Peter started guiltily. Everyone was looking at her and one or two girls were clapping.

The head's voice seemed to come from a great distance as she repeated:

"Upper School Essay Prize . . . Petronella Sterling."

Not until she was back in her seat again did she realize that her prize was that most precious of all books—*Bevis*, by Richard Jeffries. She had not thought about the essay for weeks, and only now did she remember that one of the subjects had been "Winter on the Hills," and that she had written many pages without difficulty. For a little she forgot her troubles in justifiable pride as Margaret and others near her reached curiously for the book.

At last there were cheers for the staff, cheers for the head, and cheers for the "leavers", and the Easter term was over, but it was not until after lunch that she was able to find time to read her other letter.

The envelope contained two documents. The first was folded several times until it was a small square upon which was inscribed a pine cone, the same sign as appeared on the back of the envelope.

The message inside was terse. It was headed "LONE PINE CLUB" and then read "Take notice. First meeting of the Club at Lone Pine Camp at two o'clock on Friday. All Members must be present. Come separately. Tell nobody. Urgent. Confidential. Destroy this.

"Signed,
"DAVID MORTON (Captain)."

Peter sighed. This was just what she had hoped would happen, and now she would be the only absent member.

The other note was written on a page from David's note-book.

"DEAR PETER," she read.

"We arranged the Lone Pine Meeting before your father told us you wouldn't be coming home for a bit. Bad luck. We're all fed up, and hope to see you soon. Your father seemed a bit depressed, and although Mother wanted you to come here, he said you had to go to some farm with an odd name the other side of the Stiperstones. Dickie says is this the mysterious farm you told us about last year? If it is, he will want to come and explore, and so shall we. Anyway, we can't run the Club without you, so buck up and write and tell us what it's like and how you're getting on. I'm going over to Hatchholt tomorrow for Sally. You don't mind me riding her, do you? By the

way, I saw Tom last night and he wanted to know when
you were coming. He'll be fed, too. Mother and Mary send
their love.

"DAVID.

"P.S.—We always said we'd explore the Stiperstones
didn't we? Write soon and let us know the chances."

There was nothing to do but make the best of it. Seven
Gates would be an adventure, anyway, and even if she
was by herself it would not be for more than a few days
before her father came back from Birmingham, and then
she would join up with the others.

So feeling a little more cheerful, she wandered off to
clean and oil her bicycle and alter her packing arrangements. She was not popular with the matron when she
told her that she must transfer some things from her already
packed trunk to her haversack.

But it was not until she was in her cubicle that night
that Peter definitely made up her mind to get the Mortons
and Tom to Seven Gates if it was in any way possible.
She was just ready for bed when Margaret slipped in and
pulled the curtain after her.

"Jolly good about the Essay prize, Peter," she said as
she sat on the edge of the bed. Such praise was unlike
Margaret, so Peter sensed that something else was coming.

"I suppose you've *got* to go to these relations of yours
tomorrow, haven't you, Peter?" she asked suddenly. "I
mean—you didn't seem very bucked about it all, and I
sort of wondered whether . . . whether you'd care to come
home with me . . . I know they would all be glad to
have you, Peter, and you could stay with us until you
can go home . . . that is, of course, if you'd really like it . . ."

Peter was quite overcome. She'd never been particularly
friendly with Margaret, but this really was decent of her,
and she told her so, but explained why she could not accept.

Margaret sighed. "All right, Peter, I just wondered. I
would have liked you to come. It would have been fun,

because my brother's in the Army now, and it's pretty gloomy at home . . . I don't have many adventures in the hols. Do you? I believe you once said you'd had the biggest adventure last summer of anyone in the school. Did you? I wish you'd tell me now. Nobody will be able to get to sleep for hours yet. What happened, Peter? Was it a romance?"

Peter laughed.

"No, it wasn't. Nothing like it. But if I tell you, you must swear never to repeat it, because we all had to promise at the time. Do you swear, Margaret?"

Margaret swore, and then sat entranced, sipping water from the tooth-glass while Peter told her the story of last summer's adventure.

"Where I live," she began, "it's so lonely that sometimes we don't often see anybody for days except the old postman. On our side of the Long Mynd Mountain there are several valleys, but on the Welsh side there are thick woods, and very few paths or roads. The next valley to ours is called Dark Hollow, and that's very lonely, and the next is the Witchend Valley with a lovely old farmhouse of the same name, and another farm called Ingles, after the man who works it. Last summer the nicest people I've ever met came to live at Witchend. Their name is Morton. Their father was in the R.A.F., and that left Mrs. Morton, their mother, who is a darling, David, my special friend, and the twins, Dickie and Mary. David is fifteen, like me, and the twins are nine. You can't imagine anything like these two. They're awfully alike, of course, but they are a super couple because they always stick up for each other, always do everything together and often seem to know exactly what the other is thinking without either of them saying a word.

"When I first saw them, they had all got lost on the hills above Dark Hollow, and Dickie had fallen in a bog. I remember Mary being *furious* with me because I said that her twin smelled when we'd fished him out! Anyway they came home with me and later we all explored the mountain, and for a little while we trailed a strange man with a knapsack. The twins were full of legends about the Stiperstones—where I'm going tomorrow—told them by a sailor they'd met on the train, and we wasted a lot of time before deciding to climb down the west side of the mountain, through a wood, to find a farm called Appledore.

"I knew that a Mrs. Thurston had taken the place, and we just went down for a rag and a drink of water. She was rather a horrid-looking woman—smart, with black hair and a bright red mouth, and always smoking, and she had a beastly manservant called Jacob. Anyway, she gave us a jolly good tea, and then took us home in her car just after we'd heard an owl hooting. Oh! I forgot to tell you the Mortons had a little black Scottie dog called Macbeth. He hated Mrs. Thurston as soon as he saw her and wouldn't go in the house.

"Then there was another boy called Tom who had come to help his uncle, Mr. Ingles, on the farm, and he joined up with us and we founded a secret society that I can't tell you about, and made a secret camp too.

"Then all sorts of odd things began to happen, and it seemed that the country was full of strangers. One day Mrs. Thurston walked over to call on Mrs. Morton, and Mary saw her kick the dog when she thought nobody else was looking. Then the twins had a terrific adventure. They found an R.A.F. pilot in the secret place, and he said he was Mrs. Thurston's nephew home on leave, and would they guide him over the hill to Appledore. When they got to the top of the Mynd they met Mrs. Thurston, who didn't recognize her nephew at all. Dickie and Mary went down with them to Appledore—I think that was because they were a bit frightened of coming home to a first-class bust up —and then I believe Jacob scared them and they ran away.

When they got to the top of the Mynd, the fog came down like it often does, and they had no idea where they were. Very sensibly they tried to walk downhill to find Appledore again, but got lost in the woods. Then they heard an aeroplane very low and then an owl hooting.

Old Jacob found them eventually, and together they answered a call for help, and discovered a man who had hurt his ankle, with a parachute still on him. He said he was a British officer practising for landing in Germany, and then Jacob led them all down to Appledore. Mrs. Thurston wouldn't take the twins home, but locked them into a bedroom. It was that same day that David came over to Hatchholt, and we saw Mrs. Thurston skulking about and taking photographs of the dam . . . I think I told you that Daddy had to look after this dam, didn't I, and that that's where we live?"

Margaret hugged her knees. "Yes! Yes!" she said excitedly.

"Anyway," Peter continued, now warming to her task, "David was suspicious of Mrs. Thurston, but Daddy said she was bird watching. That night, after I'd gone to bed, I heard horses coming up the valley, and it was some men with the news that the twins were lost. They said that Mr. Ingles and Tom, and David too, had gone off on a motor bike and sidecar to Appledore, but that we were to search the mountain. The fog had cleared now, so Daddy and I joined the search party and I went on Sally, the pony. On the top of the hill I met a man called Evans who said he was on a walking holiday and offered to help us. Of course we didn't find the twins 'cos they were at Appledore. After a bit, Daddy and I went home and Mr. Evans came with us, and slept downstairs because we've only got two bedrooms.

"In the morning, the Home Guard came and woke me up early. When I got downstairs, Mr. Evans had gone. They all seemed rather annoyed about it, and got me to go over to Witchend because the others had rescued the twins successfully and got them down out of their bedroom window at Appledore.

"Later that morning we were all going back to Hatchholt. I was in front with David and Sally, when the man Evans jumped up out of the heather, grabbed the pony and dashed back down the valley. Then there was a frightful roar and a crash, and I knew the dam of the reservoir had been blown up and that all the water was rushing down and would drown us if we didn't climb up the sides out of the way. We shouted to Tom and the twins who were behind us, and David and I clambered up on a big rock just in time. I had trained Sally to obey my whistle, so when I saw some Home Guards coming up the valley, I whistled in a special way, and she stopped suddenly and threw Evans over her head, right at the feet of one of the men, who hauled him off. The twins and Tom climbed up safely out of the way of the flood, and when the water had gone down, we went up to the cottage, where we found that Daddy was all right.

"When it was all worked out, we discovered that David was right. Mrs. Thurston was a German spy and all the strange men were spies dropped from aeroplanes at night, and their job was to destroy dams all over Wales and the Midlands. The twins' pilot officer was one of them of course, and so was the man we'd seen on the first day, and so was that old beast Jacob, but Evans was the worst and had actually blown up our dam . . . Anyway, it's mended now, and that was the end of that adventure . . . But it was super, wasn't it? Sometimes I wish we could have it all over again, but I'm glad I wasn't the twins lost in the fog that night. They were the real heroes . . . and my friend David, of course," she added hurriedly, going a little pink.

"Peter!" Margaret gasped incredulously. "Peter! You honestly mean to say that all that happened *last summer*, and that you've not told any of us? You mean to say that nobody in the school *knows*?"

Peter shook her head.

"Of course I didn't say anything. How could I? We all promised Captain Ward that we wouldn't talk about it, and now I've broken my promise to him by talking to you, and I feel horrid about it."

She turned fiercely on the wide-eyed Margaret, and gripped her shoulders.

"And you must swear again not to tell a soul. If ever I find out that you've said a word I'll . . . I'll scrag you," she finished lamely.

The chatter in the dormitory was dying down now. Peter and Margaret had to whisper.

"Thanks again for asking me home," Peter said, "but I shall be all right. I don't expect it will be long before Dad comes back and then we shall all be together again. . . . And you never know, Margaret . . . P'raps I might find some adventures at the place I'm going to. P'raps I'm the sort of person that adventures happen to, as Dickie would say. Good-bye, Margaret. I hope you have a lovely hols. I'll be off before breakfast, and hope I'll be at the farm by lunch time. Cook cut me some sandwiches . . . 'Bye!"

The other girl slipped off the bed.

"There's a million questions I want to ask you, Peter," she said pleadingly. "Can't you tell me what happened to those twins in Appledore and how David and those others rescued them. Come on, Peter, it's early yet . . ?"

But at this moment the dormitory door opened, and their housemistress uttered a few brief threats as to what would happen if there was any more talking or noise. When she had gone, Margaret emerged from under Peter's bed and slipped away to her own. Then someone padded over to the window and took down the blackout, and, as she lay back, Peter now could look over the top of her cubicle and see the stars.

From far away came the sound of an engine's whistle, and she pictured the train swinging over the points outside Shrewsbury Station and meandering down the vale between the Stretton Hills to home . . .

2. The Caravan

PETER WOKE with that same tight feeling in her throat. Why did she feel so excited? Then she remembered school was over.

An hour later, as she cycled down the drive with her knapsack snug between her shoulders, Margaret and two others called "Good-bye" to her from the dormitory window. Then she swung out of the lodge gates, waved to the old gardener, and the holidays had really begun.

The mist was still hanging a little low in the old streets of the town as she made for the Minsterly road and on into open country. After a few miles the road ran through a pine wood, and here she felt hungry for the first time for two days. She pulled her cycle in to the bank, climbed through a wire fence, and unbuckled the haversack. Cook had excelled herself, so she settled back comfortably against the trunk of a tree. The smell reminded her of the woods above Appledore, and she wondered what the other Lone Piners were doing now. And this gave her an idea. She fumbled in the haversack again and found a writing pad and pencil.

"DEAR DAVID"—she wrote and then added—"And all.

"Thanks for writing. I'm sorry about the meeting but it can't be helped. I've got to go to this place but I'm going to plan for you all to come too. Be ready for a special message and warn Tom as well. Take care of Sally. I'm writing this in a wood on my way to Seven Gates. Tell Dickie I remember about the Stiperstones and maybe I'll need the Lone Piners to help me.

"Love to your mother and all from

PETER".

Then she went to sleep and was wakened by the sound of rumbling wheels and cheerful singing. The sun was well up now and, rubbing her eyes, she ran to the edge of the wood. Up the road from Shrewsbury came a gaily painted caravan. A real Romany house on wheels! Red and yellow were the sides and yellow and red the wheels. The roof was green and so were the shafts, and there were white lace curtains in the windows. On the driving seat was an olive-skinned woman with a bright handkerchief round her hair, and next to her rode a serious little girl of nine. Smoke curled from the tiny chimney as the caravan passed, and Peter waved a greeting. The woman smiled with a flash of white teeth, but the girl stared straight ahead.

The doors at the back of the van were open, and there, sitting with his legs dangling above the road, was the handsomest, jolliest gipsy Peter had ever seen. He was singing, and there was laughter in his eyes and round his mouth, and golden ear-rings swung from his ears. He was not young, and he did not look very clean, but he was the happiest, most carefree thing Peter had seen for days. She could not help laughing at him when he looked up and caught her eye as she stood on the bank above him.

"It's a lovely morning," she called.

"Aye," he grinned. "It's the morning to be on the road." Then, as she waved, "Good luck, little *chi* . . ."

Peter sighed as she turned back into the wood. She looked at her watch and saw that it was nearly eleven. She had slept for a long time but she did not feel like hurrying. Even so she caught up with the caravan just on the outskirts of Pontesbury. But it took her a few minutes to find the Post Office and buy a stamped envelope for David, and had she realized that she was not likely to be at Seven Gates for lunch. She wondered if she was dawdling a bit because she did not want to go.

Outside the town the road began to climb and, six or seven miles away to the east, Peter saw the rolling grandeur of her own mountain, the Long Mynd. She did not often see it from this side, where its contours were unbroken by the deep valleys, but she could see the purple pine woods in shadow above Appledore, while the sun shone on the still brown bracken and heather on the tableland above. On her left, but nearly due south now, rose the great bulk of the Stiperstones crowned with the black, sinister quartzite rocks of the Devil's Chair.

This was a different mountain—not smooth, rolling and mysterious like the Mynd, but grim, gloomy and cruel. Peter knew there were countless legends and stories about the Stiperstones, and she remembered how she had told Dickie and Mary that the Devil's Chair is empty only when it is visible, but that when it is hidden in the clouds, or by the mists that so suddenly come down in this wild country, then Satan has taken his seat on his throne.

It was getting hot now, and she was glad enough when the hill became too steep for cycling. She was just fixing her haversack more comfortably, when she heard a frightful clatter behind her. Fifty yards farther up the hill, the road turned sharply to the left. The corner was particularly dangerous, as the woods came right down to the road, and it was impossible to see either in front or behind. Some pigeons fluttered in fright from the tree tops as the noise increased, and Peter pulled her cycle into the left and waited to see the cause of the disturbance. She might have guessed. A huge, grey tank came roaring up the hill, and as it swung towards her to take the corner a young officer, half out of the conning tower, grinned and touched his black beret to her.

The noise had hardly died away at the top of the hill when Peter, still just below the turn in the road, thought she heard a distant shout of alarm. She listened carefully, and then, quite unmistakably, came the sound of clattering hooves.

Peter knew that an experienced rider does not gallop a horse down a metalled road. With horror she realized that the caravan had probably been overtaken by the tank, but even as she slung her bicycle into the hedge and ran forward, she wondered why the horse should bolt *down* the hill in the direction from which it had come.

It was the caravan.

As she turned the corner, she noticed with relief that the road directly ahead was fairly level, but the scared horse was coming straight towards her at a pace which showed no signs of slackening. The little gipsy girl was standing on the driving seat tugging with all her strength on the reins, while the caravan lurched from one side of the road to the other. Peter knew that if she could not stop it before it got to the corner it would probably overturn.

She did not have time to feel particularly frightened, but as she ran forward she did hope that nothing was coming up the hill behind her. The child was not strong enough to check the runaway. Peter grabbed at the horse's head and as she jumped, she remembered instinctively to try to keep clear of the shafts. Then her arms were nearly jerked out, and her legs swung clear of the ground as her hands gripped the bridle and the horse reared in surprise. Tugging with all her strength she forced the horse's head down and she felt her feet touch the ground again as the caravan swung over to the left and hit the bank.

Peter hung on and tried to turn her head to see how near they were to the corner. They were perilously close, but the horse, now blowing pitiably, and with wildly rolling eyes, was coming to his senses. Peter's right arm did not seem to belong to her, but she held on grimly even though her body swung back and hit the shaft. At last she got her feet properly onto the road, and ran with the terrified horse as its canter slowed to a trot. On the very brink of the hill, it stopped and Peter let go.

For a moment or two her legs would not support her and she had to lean against the bank. She was trembling violently, and looking up she saw that the pony was doing the same. After a little, Peter stood up, felt herself all over, and noticed that her left shoe was split and her right knee bleeding.

Then she turned to the horse. Peter had a way with horses. She put her hand on his muzzle and patted him with the other and soothed him with her voice. He turned and nuzzled at her arm and gradually his trembling stopped. Then she led him forward a few steps, and the caravan lurched off the verge to the level of the road. She was just about to turn him when the gispy reached them. His face was white under the sunburn and he was too breathless to speak. He held his hand to his side and tried to smile as the little girl went up to him and started to chatter in what Peter imagined to be Romany.

They made an odd group. The sunshine dappled the road through the overhanging trees and picked out the bright colours of the caravan. The pony, his coat now black with sweat, stood quietly enough with Peter's hand still on the bridle. Peter herself felt rather awkward and shy, and was aware of the blood trickling down her leg on to her socks, and also that her shorts were covered with dirt and that tomorrow she would have a bruise as big as a dinner plate on her left thigh.

When the child had finished her story, the man came forward with dignity, and said: "You have done much for us. It was well and bravely done, and you will come with us please, so that the child's mother may pay you honour too . . ." Before she could answer he took the horse's head from her and turned him in the road. Then he examined the harness and the wheels and shafts of the caravan before opening the door at the back. Peter peeped in, and was astonished to see so little disturbance. The man saw that the stove was safe and then asked Peter to bring over her bicycle.

"Oh, but I must be getting on now, thanks awfully," she said. "I was only going to push the bike to the top of the hill, and that's not far, is it? . . . *Please* don't keep on about it, Mr.? Mr.?"

"My name is Reuben. You should call me Reuben."

"Well, all right, Mr. Reuben," Peter went on. "It was your little girl who was so brave. She hung on by herself and all I did was jump for his head when I saw him coming. I couldn't really help it 'cos I couldn't very well get out of the way . . . and besides," she added inconsequently, "I love horses and he was so frightened. It was that tank, I suppose?"

He nodded. "Yes. But you will ride up the hill with us." So Peter picked up her bicycle, and Reuben lifted it into the caravan and closed the door. Then he showed her how to climb up to the driving seat and waited until she was seated there in state before he took the horse's head and started up the hill.

"Won't your little girl come up here too?" Peter called, feeling a little ridiculous and rather enthroned. He shook his head and spoke a few words to the child, who glanced back at Peter with a slow, shy smile, and then trotted off ahead of them up the hill.

Peter's knee was painful and she felt sick. She leaned back and closed her eyes as Reuben looked over his shoulder and said gently:

"Ride at ease, little *chi*. The *romni* will clean the knee. See; she comes to meet us."

Peter opened her eyes. At the top of the hill, where the trees thinned out and the sunshine spilled in a golden flood across the road, the gipsy woman came running. Then Reuben began to talk again, and from far away Peter realized that he was telling her how the caravan had been turned at the top of the hill and that Fenella —so that was the child's name—had been left alone on the driving seat while he went to find wood and his wife went on into the quarry to see what other Romanies were camping there.

It was all rather confusing and Peter could not really understand because she felt so wretched. The horse plodded on up the hill until they met Fenella and her mother, who ran forward and grabbed her hand and kissed it. Peter was rather afraid she was going to disgrace herself. She could not say much, and when she looked down at the white road shimmering in the sun everything went hazy and she had to grab the side of the caravan to keep herself from slipping off. Dimly she realized that the woman had climbed up beside her and was holding her with an arm round her shoulders. Then the caravan lurched forward, turned the corner at the top of the hill, and swayed off the road on to a rutted lane. Peter had a dim recollection of a crowd of strange, dark faces; of a flickering fire and of towering walls of rock before she slumped sideways and felt herself lifted through the air.

Something cold was trickling down her chest . . . somebody was smacking her hand . . . water was on her face and lips . . . Her head was resting on something warm and soft. She stirred and struggled to sit up. Reuben was on his knees in front of her with an enamel mug of water poised for another throw. There was a smell of wood smoke and a babble of voices. Wide-eyed, Fenella was on her other side, and then a soft voice behind her said, "Good! You are better now. Drink this."

She never knew what she did drink, but it was tea of some sort—scalding, brown, sweet and yet scented! A magic gipsy tea, she thought, as her head cleared and the sickness passed. Then she realized that Fenella's mother was supporting her firmly but gently, and she sipped gratefully again at the steaming potion. It was lovely. The warmth seeped through her and she felt ravenously hungry as the smell of something luscious mingled with wood and smoke drifted towards her. She laughed a little shakily and sat up.

She was in a huge quarry in which four other gipsy caravans were already at rest. The ground was marked with the black circles of burnt-out fires which seemed to show that this was an established camping ground. She tried to bend her knee and winced, and Reuben said:

"You are better now. You are a brave *chi*. We shall not forget. Now you must stay and eat, and then if you wish you shall spend the night with us . . . But you must not go on until you have eaten . . . it is *hotchi-witchi* . . . very good . . . what is it, you ask? . . . The Gentiles call him hedge-pig . . . And you must not go on until the knee is clean."

Peter could not see what it was in the tin that her hostess fetched from the caravan, but it looked as if it was dried herbs. As the Reubens' fire had not been lit long, Fenella was sent over to another camp for boiling water, and then Mrs. Reuben concocted some sort of mess with the herbs and the water and some powder out of a dirty-looking medicine bottle.

Peter began to feel rather apprehensive, and thought of the hygienic "surgery" at Pollards and matron's antiseptic precautions, as the gipsy approached with a small basin. However, she realized how she would upset her new friends if she declined the treatment, and with the thought that she could wash off all the mess as soon as she got away, she tried to smile gratefully as the hot paste from the basin was spread over the cut. It stung at first, but after a few minutes the pain went and she found that she could move the knee without much trouble.

She felt curiously lazy. She knew she ought to be getting on to Seven Gates, but she was thrilled with her new friends and looking forward to the hedgehog.

After a little, Fenella called shrilly—"*Hotchi-witchi* . . . ready . . ." and Mrs. Reuben turned to Peter.

"Come and see."

They went over together to an orange caravan under the trees and the woman said:

"Miranda—you must call me that—is in your debt. She will not forget. Reuben and Miranda and Fenella are your friends now. Tell us what you are named and where you come from and where you go. But wait. Tell us when you have eaten. See—here is our hedge-pig."

Peter stood by and watched the other gipsies rake away the hot embers of their wood fire, until two cylinders of baked clay were exposed. Fenella ran for a dish from the Reubens' van and one of the glowing cylinders was poked onto it. Then, with mutual expressions of goodwill, the cooks and the Reubens with their guest parted.

Round their own fire, Peter watched how the baked clay was cracked and peeled off, bringing with it the spines of the hedgehog and leaving him bare and beautifully cooked. From the pot then came a stew of gravy and vegetables, a generous helping of which was piled onto the plate of the guest of honour. She did not see how Reuben divided up the hedgehog, but her share was certainly tasty—something between rabbit and chicken— and she was so hungry that she finished her plateful almost as soon as Fenella.

Then Reuben sighed loudly and felt for his pipe. Fenella dipped her bread into the pot for the last time, and then, like a kitten, curled up on the grass and went peacefully to sleep. Miranda leaned back against the wheel of the caravan, shook her ear-rings, smiled at Peter and said:

"Tell me, my pretty one, what are you called, so that the Romany will know their friend again. Tell us, too, where are you going?"

"My name is Petronella. Most people call me Peter——"

"That is a pity. Petronella! That is as good as a Romany name. Tell us some more, and then, if you wish it, I shall look at your hand and tell you more of yourself than you know. You have a handsome, lucky face, my pretty Petronella!"

Peter blushed. She did not really want her fortune told, and it was embarrassing to be spoken to in this way by this fine-looking woman, who, half the time, seemed to know what she was thinking before she spoke. Now she laughed merrily. "Never mind, little one. Perhaps in a year or two you will want to hear what Miranda can tell you of the future . . . Reuben," she called. "Come here. Our friend tells us where she goes and who she is."

So Peter told them easily enough of school and of her home at Hatchholt and finished up by saying:

"I'm on my way now to Barton Beach by the Stiper-stones. I've got an uncle and aunt there. Do you know where it is? It's a farm called Seven Gates."

Reuben gasped suddenly and dropped the stick he was

whittling. Miranda looked up at him in surprise. "Is that the big house by the place they call Black Dingle?" He nodded. Then to Peter. "And is it your uncle that lives there and you go to him now—today?"

"Yes," she said. "Mr. Micah Sterling is my uncle's name. But why do you look like that? Is anything wrong? Do you really know the farm and my uncle? And if so, why do you look so strangely at each other?"

Then they tried to put her off until she became almost frightened because she did not know why they seemed reluctant to talk about Seven Gates. At last Reuben took his pipe from his mouth and smiled down at her.

"Listen, little *chi*. You are our friend so we will tell you why we are not happy that you are going to this place. We Romany do not like the Stiperstone country. Our wise ones tell us it is the oldest country in England. Those black rocks we call the Devil's Chair stood once above the ice that covered all this land. There is much that is bad on that mountain, and although we know this country well and sell many baskets round these villages, the Stiperstones we hate. Remember, Petronella, our friend, never to be seen near the Stiperstones on the longest night in the year, for then all the ghosts in Shropshire and all the counties beyond meet on the summit—right on and around the Chair they meet—to choose their king . . . And any who venture out on that night and see the ghosts of all the years' dead from hereabouts are stricken with fear and often do not live the year . . . And that, we know, is true . . . And you ask about your uncle? I do not know him. We do not often go that way, for his farm is in the very shadow of the evil mountain and hard against a lonely, rocky valley called Black Dingle. Once, long ago, we went there to sell baskets, but the house was empty, and it seemed no woman lived there then. Doubtless your uncle is a good man, my pretty, but 'tis said he is a hard one and lonely, too."

His wife broke in.

"You are too young for that old place, with all its gates

and doors. Rather stay with us for a little and Miranda will teach you to cook hedge-pig, to make baskets, and to tell the future, too."

"I've got to go," Peter said; "but thank you very much all the same for asking me to stay. I ought to start because the sun has gone in and I believe it's going to rain . . . But I do hope to see you all again. And I've got some friends who'd love to meet you, too. P'raps we could arrange it one day . . . Ah! and when you come the Long Mynd way, don't forget to come and see me at Hatchholt—if it's holidays, of course—and the others are at Witchend. Do you know those places?"

Reuben smiled. "We know them. We will come."

Miranda came up to her and took her hand.

"Good-bye, my little *chi*. We shall meet again. Good luck go with you. But you will have the luck, for I see it in your hand, as I see the beauty in your face. One day you will have your heart's desire, but there are many adventures to come first . . . The Romany never forget. Miranda and Reuben will always remember what you have done for them this day."

So Peter waved to the other gipsies in the quarry and pushed her cycle out into the road.

"Well," said Peter to herself, "I never thought gipsies were as nice as that. They were a bit dirty, but they were fun . . . I wonder what my fortune would have been . . . P'raps I was silly not to let Miranda tell it . . . Oh, dear, now I've got to go and find gloomy old Seven Gates, I suppose . . ."

The road rushed downhill now and Peter sped between the darkening woods with the wind piling up the clouds behind her. The lovely foretaste of spring which the morning's sun had brought was forgotten. When she pedalled through the next village the road was spattered with raindrops, and, high up on her left, the lonely Stiperstone range loomed menacingly over the cottages and tiny church. Peter shivered. She hated the journey now.

Then the worst happened. Her back wheel bumped and,

when she got off to investigate, the tyre was flat. There was nothing to do but to try and mend the puncture, and feeling that this was just what *would* happen today, Peter turned her bicycle up by the ditch and felt in her saddlebag for the puncture set. It was not there. She looked again, without luck. As the rain increased, she went through her haversack. Then she remembered that a girl at school had borrowed it three days before.

Peter had had a big day, but there seemed no alternative to a long walk. The knapsack seemed to weigh a ton, but she plodded on doggedly, and at last saw the welcome white gleam of a signpost ahead where a narrow lane branched off to the left towards the mountain. "Barton Beach 2 miles," it read.

After a little she heard behind her the sound of someone whistling and the clop of horses' hooves. She was so tired now that she willingly waited to see what was coming. Round the corner of the lane came an ancient horse and trap driven by a red-headed girl of about twelve, who pulled up when she saw Peter.

Peter rather liked what she saw, for the girl had a good-natured freckled face, with a snub nose. She smiled, but did not speak.

"I say," Peter said, "could you give me a lift to Barton Beach? I've got a puncture and I've walked simply miles. . . . D'you think we could hoist the bike up on the back?"

"What are you going to Barton for?" the girl asked slowly.

Peter reddened. "To see my uncle, if you must know, but if you can't give me a lift don't bother. I can walk."

"You must be the girl coming to Seven Gates," was the reply.

"How do you know where I am going, and what's it to do with you?"

"Oh, don't get in a bate," the other went on calmly. "My Mum keeps the post office and we know everything. There was a telegram about you . . . Jump up—oh, wait a sec. I'll help you haul up the bike."

And this was the way in which Peter rode into Barton Beach. The girl's name was Jenny, she soon discovered, and she was rather solemn and rather fun, but very inquisitive.

"I'll have to take old George to the stable when we get home," she said, "and then I'll show you the way to Seven Gates. It will be dark early tonight, and it's not easy to find . . . Fancy old Mr. Sterling being your uncle! Gosh! that's funny."

Peter asked why.

"Nobody here knew he was an uncle, and even if he is yours, I'd better tell you that I wouldn't be in your shoes for anything."

"Why not? What's the matter with him?"

"Well, I wouldn't want to stay in that great ugly house, anyway, and I don't like it up there on the mountain."

"Yes, but what's the matter with Uncle?"

Jenny tried to laugh it off.

"Oh, I didn't mean anything is the *matter* with him . . . We don't see him walking about the village now. Some say he goes out a lot at night by himself, walking over the hills. . . . But I don't know really . . . What have you come here for?"

Peter explained that she had come for part of her holidays, but it did sound rather silly on a cold, damp, dark evening like this. It didn't seem as if anyone could possibly come for a *holiday* to such a place.

"Oh, well," Jenny said, "I have to help a bit in the shop and run errands like this, too, but perhaps we could have some fun together here. Now we're really home, and I'll just tell Mum I'm back and then we'll go up to Seven Gates."

They had come now to a long, straggling village street, and old George broke into a shambling trot as he scented his stable. Jenny pulled him up and lowered the bicycle to Peter, who leaned it against an old-fashioned, dirty-looking shop, which had a letter-box at the side of one window. Above the door she could just read "*General* HARMAN *Stores*."

"Better wait inside," Jenny called as she followed the horse round into the yard.

As Peter opened the door she was startled by a horrible clanging above her head. She looked up in alarm at the rusty swinging bell, and then a sharp voice called from somewhere in the gloom at the back:

"Who's there?" called the voice. "Go away. I can't serve you. We're closed."

Peter was still wondering what to answer when Jenny's voice came also from the hidden back regions. "It's all right, Mum. It's a friend of mine called Peter. She's the girl coming to Seven Gates."

"Good gracious! Why didn't you say so? Come in here, child, and let's have a look at you."

There was another clanking and a heavy curtain at the back of the shop was pulled aside to disclose a cosy, lamp-lit sitting-room and a little shrew-like woman with grizzled hair. Feeling rather like an exhibit in a museum and very tired and grubby as well, Peter advanced into the lamp-light.

"Humph!" Mrs. Harman grunted. "Look as if you want a wash. What's that mess all over your knee?"

But Peter was weary of answering questions and wanted to get on. She knew she was late, and that, whether she liked them or not, her aunt and uncle would wonder what had happened to her. So she answered as politely as she could, and just as Jenny came into the room, said, "And it's good of Jenny to show me the way—I've got an awful puncture, and that's really why I'm so late."

"Jenny's not going with you to Seven Gates," old Mrs. Harman said sharply. "I won't have my girl going there—not for anything, I won't, and that's flat!"

Peter felt the tears of humiliation sting her eyes. These questions and little mysteries about Seven Gates and the Stiperstones were all so silly; angrily she turned her back to the lamplight and walked out through the shop with her head held high. Anyway, Uncle Micah was *her* uncle, whether other people liked it or not. It was her business and nobody else's. She hated old Mrs. Harman.

The bell jangled fiercely behind her as she tripped on the worn step and went over to her bicycle. It was dusk now, but the rain had stopped and, over to the west, a few angry bars of orange and red showed where the sun was going down behind the driven storm clouds. She had no idea which way to go, but at that moment the door of an inn on the other side of the street opened and a fat man came out on the doorstep.

"Good evening," Peter called. "Can you tell me the way to Seven Gates, please?"

The man looked at her curiously.

"Of course I can, missie. Straight on up the hill, second lane on your right. Go along the lane till you come to a thick wood. Half a mile farther on there's a white gate on your left leading into the wood. That's the first of the white gates . . . But you'd better hurry, lass. It'll be dark quick tonight." Then he paused and seemed to smile. "Are you stopping there the night, lass?"

More questions! But Peter liked him. He was nice. "Yes. Mr. Sterling is my uncle. Good-bye, and thanks awfully," and she plodded up the way he was pointing. She had just left the last of the houses when again she heard running footsteps behind her.

"Peter," a voice called breathlessly. "Peter. Wait for me. It's Jenny. I've come to show you the way."

Peter turned her back.

"I can manage, thank you," she said coldly. "No need for you or your mother to bother," and she walked on.

"Peter, don't be a beast. Wait for me. I've run away specially."

Perhaps she was being rather a beast after all.

"Sorry, Jenny. I'm feeling grumpy. It was decent of you to come, though, but I think I can find my way. Why wouldn't your mother let you come?"

But Jenny would not answer the last question. All she said was:

"If you leave your bike in this field I'll collect it on my way back and get your puncture mended in the morning. I promise I will, and then you needn't push it along now."

This was certainly a good idea, and when Jenny insisted on carrying the knapsack for a little Peter felt very ashamed of her bad manners. Soon they came to the second lane, and when they had turned down it, Peter said again:

"It's jolly good of you to come, Jenny. Will you get into trouble when you get back? Why didn't your mother want you to come with me?"

"Oh—I expect I will. I'm always getting into trouble. I wish I could go away to school like you do—I hate it here. I hate this place. Will you come and get your bike tomorrow and come and see me?"

"'Course I will. I'd like to. There'll be nobody at Seven Gates of my age. And you must come up there. I'll ask Aunt Carol to ask you."

"I don't expect Mum would let me do that—but we'll meet somehow, Peter. It'll be grand."

They had reached the wood now and the whispering trees shut out the twilight of the stormy evening. In another ten minutes it would be quite dark.

Suddenly Jenny stopped.

"I can't come any farther," she said sharply, but with an odd break in her voice. "I must go back at once. You're nearly at the first gate, and when you're there you just follow the track. Good-bye, Peter—and good luck!" she added unexpectedly, and before she could be thanked she had turned and was running back down the lane.

Peter trudged on till she came to a big white gate. There was a notice on it in crude red letters—"STRICTLY PRIVATE". The gate was stiff and the hinges screamed as she opened it. Two bats fluttered round her head as she turned up the track. She was so tired now that her legs did not seem to belong to her. She could feel the bruise on her hip, her head ached and she was lonely and a little frightened. The rising wind made an odd rustling sound in the tree tops which bent towards her and made an arch over the path up which she blundered. Peter hated feeling closed in. She was used to the wild, open moorland of the Long Mynd, but here, in these beastly whispering trees, she felt as if the huge bulk of the Stiperstones was going to fall on her.

Then she came to the second gate. This was white, too, but there was barbed wire on the top and she scratched her hand.

Suddenly she heard the sound of someone singing, and ahead, down the track, she thought she caught the gleam of a torch. The clear and lovely voice came weirdly through the dark and Peter's spirits rose. That voice was just what she needed. She hunched the knapsack up on her back, squared her shoulders and held up her chin, determined to arrive at Seven Gates with her colours flying. Then abruptly the singing stopped and a woman's voice called, "Is anyone there?"

"Yes, there is," Peter answered. "It's me, and I can't see where I am."

The voice came nearer. "Is it Petronella? My dear, what *has* happened to you? We were beginning to get so worried. It's too dark for us to see each other, but I'm your Aunt Carol. Come along and let's get home quickly, for you must be tired out."

What happened next was all very bewildering. Peter could not really see her new aunt, but the hand tucked into her arm was firm, strong and friendly.

Then they passed through another white gate into what seemed to be an enormous farmyard. Now that they were out of the gloom of the wood, there was just enough grey twilight for Peter to see a group of cottages on the left, while in front was a gaunt, austere brick house. Beyond that and to her right was the shadowy bulk of great barns.

Aunt Carol, whom Peter could now see was not much taller than herself, looked at her and said: "You've been here before, haven't you? Do you remember it?"

Peter was puzzled. "I seem to remember the house." She looked up and shivered instinctively. "And I remember the mountain up there."

Then her heart banged uncomfortably as her aunt opened the door. Now for Uncle Micah.

An oil-lamp was burning in a little table in the bare-looking hall, but her aunt led her straight down a stone passage to the kitchen, where a fire was glowing between the bars of a gigantic range. Aunt Carol reached up and turned up the wick of another lamp hanging from the ceiling.

"Now let's look at each other," she said with a laugh. "My word, Petronella, but you're not much like the Sterlings. More like your mother, I should say. But you look worn out. What *have* you been doing to yourself? . . . And that great lump of a knapsack! Slip it off, my dear. You're home now, and a cup of tea is what you need!"

Then, for the second time that day, poor Peter felt dazed, and for a minute the room swayed round her. She shut her eyes and waited until the horrid feeling passed and then slipped her knapsack from her shoulders and sat down. Her aunt was looking at her keenly.

"What's wrong, my dear?"

Peter gulped. "I'm so tired, Aunt Carol. I had a puncture and had to walk miles, and then this morning I got mixed up with gipsies and . . . oh, Auntie, could I go to bed, d'you think?"

"You can do what you like," was the surprising reply, and then, before she could collect her thoughts, this extremely nice aunt put one arm round her waist, hoisted up the knapsack with the other and led her up a dark and depressing staircase.

"Here's your room, my dear! If you haven't brought a dressing-gown, I'll lend you one. Get out of those grubby things as quickly as you can and have a hot bath."

When she got back from the bathroom her aunt was putting a hot-water bottle in the bed. On the chest of drawers was a loaded tray and Peter suddenly felt hungry and realized that the hedgehog in the quarry was a long time ago.

"Better now?" Her aunt smiled. "While you're having your supper you can tell me what you've been up to."

Peter snuggled thankfully into bed and looked at the boiled egg and brown bread and butter with enthusiasm. And the tea was nice and weak, and Aunt Carol had brought a cup for herself and sat on the end of the bed and sipped it.

Peter had time to look at her properly now. She was certainly nice and nearly pretty, with a lovely smile and big brown eyes. Her dark hair was parted at the side, but could not hide a broad streak of almost white hair that ran across her head, giving her a rather startling appearance. Her hands, Peter noticed, were worn with work.

She smiled steadily over her tea-cup and said:

"Now what's all this about gipsies?"

So Peter told her story as modestly as she could, and twice Aunt Carol said "Good girl," and once "That was sensible," but when Peter got to the part about Mrs. Harman in the shop, she laughed and said:

"Oh! she's just a stupid old woman! I'm sorry for little Jenny—I believe she's unkind to her . . . You'd better ask Jenny up here, while you're with us . . . but I doubt if she'll come," she added, half to herself.

When Peter had finished both her story and her supper, she plucked up her courage and said:

"Where's Uncle Micah? I haven't seen him yet."

A shadow passed over her aunt's face.

"Oh, he's out. He had to go out. Perhaps he's gone to look for you. I think he was getting worried."

Then she sat down on the bed again and took Peter's left hand in her own.

"Petronella," she began, "I ought to tell you that sometimes your uncle does rather unusual things. You must try not to be surprised or frightened at what he says or does, because he grieves a lot. I am glad you have come and I hope you won't be bored here. I've wanted you to come for a long time because it is good for him to have young people round him and . . . and you see, my dear, people here—the cottage people and others—don't understand him. You mustn't mind if sometimes he doesn't seem to be listening to you or if he's a bit snappy . . . And, besides, he's very proud of you . . ."

"*Proud* of me?" said Peter in bewilderment. "*Proud of me?* Why, he can't remember me—and doesn't know anything about me."

"Oh, yes, he does. Your father tells him everything about you and your school . . . He ought to, Petronella. He has a right to know how you are getting on."

"Why?" the startled girl asked.

"Why? Don't you know? He pays your school fees. That's why you are able to go to the Castle School. After Charles went he wanted you to have this chance, but if your father hasn't told you he ought to have done."

Peter didn't know who Charles was, but she was up in arms in a flash for her father.

"Perhaps Daddy did tell me. I forget. But, anyway, it doesn't matter. If he didn't there's a jolly good reason for it, you can be sure."

"Well," her aunt smiled, "that's why your uncle wants to see you, anyhow. You won't see him till the morning now, so you'd better go to sleep."

Then she kissed her lightly, tucked her up—and this was a new experience for Peter—and turned out the lamp.

"What a day!" Peter thought as she turned over.

Outside the wind moaned in the trees and a pale moon came up behind the Stiperstones. Downstairs the mistress of Seven Gates took a saucepan off the fire for the fifth time and somewhere out in this wild and desolate country the master strode lonely through the night.

3. The Seven Gates

THE RUMBLE of men's voices woke Peter early on her first morning at Seven Gates.

A grey square of light showed her the window, so she slipped out of bed and looked out into the farmyard towards the two ugly cottages which she had seen the evening before. It was early enough to be misty but two shadowy figures and a monster, which she supposed to be a horse, explained the voices.

The house was very quiet as she dressed quickly and stole down the stairs. There was a door into the yard from the scullery and she drew the bolts quietly and slipped out into the mist.

Away on the left were some fields which sloped away into the hazy distance. The big farmyard was bounded by a brick wall and, from where she was standing, she could see two more white gates. But over all towered the bulk of the mountain, the lower slopes of which were covered with heather. From where she was standing the Devil's Chair was invisible, but she knew it was there—poised high above the house—and now, no doubt, "he" was on his throne. She ran back to the wall and looked up to satisfy her curiosity. She was right. The Chair was hidden in the mist.

Then she heard the voices again, and walked over to the corner of the yard. The mist was thinning now as the sun gained strength and she was able to see the two men by the horse trough before they noticed her. For some reason she thought instantly of Snow White's Seven Dwarfs, although one of these men was tall and thin and the other short and stumpy. They were arguing about something as the big horse between them sucked up his morning drink.

Peter heard the one she thought of as Grumpy say in an unexpectedly thin little voice:

"I sin him, I tells yer. I sin him from upstairs windy . . . down foot of Dingle."

The other then noticed Peter and nudged his fellow dwarf and both swung round to stare at her. Peter grinned disarmingly.

"Good morning," she said. "It's going to be a lovely day, isn't it? I got up early specially to see you. Do you both live in those cottages?"

Instead of answering, Grumpy squeaked:

"And who might you be, Miss?"

Peter explained while they both stared at her incredulously. Then—"Dang me," said the tall one, "dang me, but be you going to stay here, Missie? You be? D'yer hear that, Humphrey? Little Miss be livin' here a while."

"Oh, well," Peter hastened to explain, "I shan't be here long. Only till my father comes to fetch me in a few days. . . . I say! Can I go everywhere and explore all those barns? And is there a pony I could ride?"

They looked at each other apprehensively, but Peter went on:

"But what are your names?" They told her they were Henry and Humphrey. Henry was Grumpy and they were soon as friendly as she had hoped, but they would not show her the barns or give her permission to explore.

"Better ask Master," they said, or "Wait till Master be come," so Peter humoured them and followed them about their leisurely work and listened to their leisurely talk. After a little she asked them about the mountain towering above them, and whether all the stories she had heard of the Devil's Chair were true, but they pretended not to have heard and she did not ask again.

There was no sign of life yet from the big house except a promising plume of smoke from the kitchen chimney, so when Henry led the old mare over to one of the white gates she ran ahead and opened it for him. She turned to wave to Humphrey, and then said briefly, "Give me a leg up," and almost before the astonished Henry could answer was up on the old mare's back. And as they ambled down a cart track which led them to fields already blue-green with autumn-sown grain, her new friend began to tell her other stories of Shropshire.

She heard how Edric the Wild—or the Forester as some called him—a few years before the coming of William of Normandy was hunting in the wild mountainous country in the Forest of Clun. He became separated from his companions and, as dusk was falling, saw a mysterious light which led him to a strange building. The light was streaming from a window, and looking through, he saw "seven beautiful maids all robed in fairest white and dancing hand in hand." Instantly he fell in love with the youngest and most beautiful of the sisters and, rushing to the door, burst it open and seized her in his arms. Then the maid's six fair sisters changed into the fiercest beasts and attacked him with tooth and claw. With his precious burden held aloft Edric fought his way out and galloped away.

For three months the lovely and mysterious wife of the wild forester spoke no word until one day she opened her lips and wished him well and promised to be true to him for all time if he never reproached her for her sisters or spoke of the place from which he had snatched her away.

Her name was Godda. They lived happily for a long time, and through all the borderland, and much of England too, her great beauty was renowned. And then one day Edric, because he was kept waiting for his meal, forgot his promise and in his rough, wild way, blamed the fair Godda for her sisters and cried: "Is it your sisters who have kept you waiting?" And at this, with a sad look of remorse Godda disappeared and he never saw her again.

But although after this Edric submitted to the Conqueror, years of war and outlawry followed and his name was a byword throughout the land.

"But 'tis said, Miss," old Henry squeaked, as he harnessed the old horse to the long roller, "that he did not die like mortal man do die. Nobody ever heard that he did die and they say that he sleeps till judgment day under these very hills. Not for Wild Edric will come the joys of resurrection morning, but only the longed-for rest o' death . . . Aye! that's what they say . . ."

"Go on," urged Peter. "You must know more than that about him? Don't people say he can be seen on these hills? Over at home on the Mynd, I 'member Mr. Ingles told me once that he comes there like a great, black dog with fiery eyes."

"Aye, maybe," said Henry tersely.

"But does he come here?" Peter persisted.

Old Henry looked at her sideways.

"Aye! He's been seen hereabouts. 'Afore the last war he was seen a-ridin' with his hell-mad hunt up the Dingle yonder . . . And there's a girl down Barton Beach seen him but a while since . . . Always he comes a'blowing of his horn when trouble's brewin' . . . Night 'afore young Humphrey's boy was took prisoner was when the girl saw him."

"What's he like?" Peter whispered. "Have *you* seen him, Mr. Henry?"

"Me? No, Missie . . . Times in winter we've heard him riding over the hills from my place yonder but I've never seen him, thank God . . . Short and dark they say he is and fierce looking and on a big white horse. And by his side now rides his fairy bride. Dressed in green she is, with golden hair a'floatin' down her back . . . 'Tis ill to see the Wild Huntsman, Missie. If ever you hear his horn 'tis well to hide your eyes till the hunt has passed you by."

"Gosh!" breathed Peter ecstatically. What a story she would have to tell the others!

She sighed, and then was awakened from her dreams by a stern and terrible voice behind her.

"Petronella!" it boomed.

"The Lord ha' mercy on us, it's the Master," squeaked Henry without turning his head.

Peter slipped from the roller and ran back down the field. Standing in the path awaiting her was Uncle Micah. She never had a moment's doubt that it was Uncle Micah and he looked much, much worse than she had imagined. Tall. Forbidding. Black clothes. Hard black hat. Big black beard. She remembered that beard—and those smouldering eyes glaring at her now as she came up to him.

"Good morning, Uncle Micah," she said politely, with hardly a quiver in her voice. "How do you do? I hope I haven't kept you waiting for breakfast. I woke up early and I've been exploring."

He did not answer but put his hands on her shoulders and looked searchingly into her face. She returned his look fearlessly, and realized almost at once that he was not so much to be feared as to be pitied.

"Come, child," he said at last. "We were perplexed," and led the way back to the farm. Peter soon discovered that her uncle invariably spoke like this but he was a man of few words, for he said nothing else until they got back. When she knew him better she realized that he *did* talk rather like the Old Testament.

The kitchen looked more cheerful in the morning sunlight, and was filled with a delicious smell of frying bacon. Aunt Carol, she thought, looked tired behind her smile of welcome, and when she ran forward to help her with the plates she whispered, "It *was* rude of me, Auntie! I'm so sorry. I forgot the time, but I got talking to Henry."

"That's all right, Peter," she answered as she stooped over the fire, "but your uncle doesn't like to be kept waiting for his meals, and he wouldn't sit down without you. How are you this morning?"

Before Peter could answer, her uncle boomed from the huge chair at the head of the table:

"Is not the meal yet prepared?"

Peter sat down thankfully. But only for a moment. A glance like black lightning from the head of the table brought her to her feet again for grace. And what a grace!

So different from the simple, sincere "Lord Bless this Food . . ." of Hatchholt, for this was a personal appeal for mercy and light from Uncle Micah to his Maker.

When at last they sat down Peter was too hungry to talk. There were boiled eggs with the bacon and fried bread. There seemed to be plenty of butter, but she noticed that the marmalade was in front of Uncle Micah, while she shared with her aunt blackberry and apple jam. Presently the black beard was wiped and the specially large cup returned to the saucer.

"Before we ask for God's guidance . . ." boomed Uncle Micah, and "Oh, gosh!" thought Peter, who, although she had skimped her washing, had *not* skimped her prayers that morning, "had I better ask him what I want now or after?" but a warning look from Aunt Carol and just the faintest suspicion of a twinkle, too—warned her that after would be better.

During the continuation of Uncle Micah's prayers, Peter, now on her knees, watched a shaft of sunlight travelling across the stone floor towards her aunt's chair. "I can't stick this on my own," she was thinking. "I just can't. I must get the others here somehow till Daddy comes." The voice droned on and the stone floor hurt, but at last "Arr-men," declaimed Uncle Micah, and after a discreet peep Peter got up and rubbed her knees.

"Oh, Uncle," she began rapidly, before he had time to be snatched up to heaven, "after I've helped Auntie may I go anywhere I want, please, and may I explore the barns?"

"Of course she can, Micah! Are your keys hanging up behind the clock if we can't find you when we're ready? I'll take Petronella round if you're busy."

Now Peter had an idea that Uncle Micah would have declined her request on the odd principle that if you want something it must be wrong, but now he gave his wife a patriarchal-like inclination of the head and said, "So be it. Should the child wish to find me later, I shall be in the thirty-acre doubtless admonishing Humphrey."

And when he had gone it seemed that the sun shone more brightly.

"Give me a hand upstairs, Peter, and we'll soon be through," said Aunt Carol. "Old Annie—she's Mrs. Henry really—will be along presently to wash these up."

She added, "I want you to be happy here, although I'm afraid it will be a bit lonely for you . . ." But before Peter could put in a hint about the absent members of the Lone Pine Club, her aunt went on:

"You don't remember Charles?"

Peter shook her head in bewilderment.

"And you didn't know your real Aunt Martha—Charles's mother? . . . Of course you wouldn't, Peter. . . . I think I ought to tell you about them. Your Aunt Martha died when you were a baby and when her son Charles was twelve. Your Uncle Micah brought Aunt Martha here as a bride, and there is a story which you must ask him to tell you one day about the seven white gates, and why he came here. After your aunt died he lived alone here with Charles for seven years. Quite alone they lived, and all the time he was grieving for Aunt Martha. Then one day Charles went away and never came back, and not until a card came nearly a year later from Canada or America did he know he was alive. And because your Uncle Micah was angry and lonely and unhappy, and because I know he is really a good man and has a kind heart, I thought someone ought to take proper care of him—and that's what I'm trying to do, my dear."

"But why did Charles go away?"

"Only your uncle knows, and he won't tell me. I think they quarrelled . . . Your uncle was never the same after his wife died, and now he says he will never forgive Charles, and yet, Peter, I know he is grieving for him. He was so proud of his son and he never stops missing him. And don't you see, Peter, that that is why he is interested in you. You are his only brother's child. Besides Charles, you are all he has of his own flesh and blood. I do so want you to try and make him forget himself and his troubles for a little."

Then Peter had her first big idea.

"Auntie! I know who would cheer Uncle up. I know just what would be good for him. The twins!"

"What twins?"

"Dickie and Mary, of course! Daddy said once that nobody could be quite the same after carrying on a conversation with the Morton twins, and I don't believe they would."

"Well, come downstairs and help me with the chicken food, and then we'll explore and you can tell me all about the marvellous twins."

So Peter told her aunt all about the Mortons, and Tom Ingles and the Lone Pine Club, and also something of the mystery of Witchend.

"And I know it's a lot to ask, Aunt Carol," she finished up. "But if only they were all here we could have the most marvellous time, and I'm sure we could cheer up Uncle Micah like anything."

"I'd love to have your friends, Peter dear, but we can't put them up. You see—there's only your room and . . . and Charles's room with furniture in."

"But we'd camp out and bring our own food . . ."

"But you can't camp out in this weather, Peter . . . But we'll think about it and see if there's a way. I'd love to meet those two."

Then they wandered round the farmyard. She saw the dark wood through which she had climbed the night before passing three white gates to get home. Then the fourth gate she had been through this morning with Henry and her uncle. The fifth was a small footpath gate behind the barns leading downhill to a little bridge over a stream. The sixth, her aunt showed her, led to the Henry and Humphrey cottages.

"And the seventh?" Peter asked.

"It isn't a gate," her aunt said. "There's a story about it, and it's something to do with Charles, but here it is. Look!" and she led the way to the corner of the yard. The barns were built in the shape of a big L, but the biggest black barn with its mellow roof of lichened tiles looked deserted, for weeds covered the ground and cobwebs were thick above the gigantic *white* double doors that stood at least eight feet high.

Peter looked round in astonishment.

"Yes," her aunt nodded. "That's the seventh white gate. Your uncle calls it Charles's barn and will not have it used. I've never seen the doors open, and I'm not quite sure why they were painted white. You must ask your uncle one day . . ."

Peter's voice began to shake with excitement.

"But what's in the barn? Is it empty? Can we look?"

"Yes," said her aunt suddenly. "We will look. I've got the keys here, and now you've come to stay we'll start to do some things we ought to have done years ago . . . There's an oil-can in the scullery . . . We shall want it for this old padlock, Peter . . . run quickly."

The moment the white doors swung back, Peter knew that her guess had been a lucky one. This was the place!

The sunlight streamed into the old barn which was vaulted and pillared like a church. The floor was of uneven brick and on the wooden walls hung the rusty relics which are always to be found on the walls of barns. There were several big wooden partitions—once used to divide the stored grain—against the left-hand wall and in the far shadows Peter could see a wooden stairway. In the farthest corner, under a window, was something that made her heart thump with excitement. She ran into the gloom, and there was a flutter of wings as dozens of startled bats blundered about into the hated light. The dust rose in clouds around her feet as she stood before an old, rusty iron cooking-stove with a black chimney disappearing through the wall above her.

"Auntie," she called, "it is a stove. And look, it's dry everywhere, and we could cook here and sleep here, too. Oh, *please*, please may we have the Lone Piners here to stay? We'd live here all the time, and we could sleep in those partitions—or upstairs if it's all right up there . . ."

and she clambered up the rickety stairway into a vast granary which stretched over the barn below. Right above the great white doors was a little window at floor level, and the moment she saw it Peter vowed that here she would sleep so that she could live above the world and watch the stars swing over the wood without moving her head from the pillow. For a moment she crouched down and looked over the gently swaying treetops away down into the valley and Barton Beach. Then she jumped up.

"Come and look, Aunt Carol! It's the most marvellous place."

And when her aunt came up she seemed to have made up her mind.

"Yes, Peter, you're right. It's a splendid place for a camp, and if your uncle agrees then I see no reason why you shouldn't have your friends here. How many did you say?"

"Well, there's three for certain—David, Dickie and Mary. And four if Tom Ingles can come. There's Macbeth—'cos I'm sure Mary won't come without him . . . Macbeth? Oh! he's a dog,—small and black, with short legs—*you* know the sort, Auntie . . . And then there's another thing. I'm sorry, but my pony Sally ought to come—she's with the Mortons now, and if Uncle didn't like her being out in a field, she could go in a stable p'raps, although she hates that . . ."

"Stop! Stop!" cried Mrs. Sterling, covering her ears. "That's more than enough—it sounds like a circus . . . Now come here and try to listen . . .

"I'd like you to have your friends here, my dear. It will be good for us all, but you must go and ask your uncle if you can use the barn as you suggest, and I don't think I should mention the dog or the pony. I should let those just arrive! And if you're a little uncertain about Tom, I wouldn't mention him either, because it makes it sound rather a lot, and it's a long time since Seven Gates had any visitors . . . If we have the time today, I'll help you clean this place up, but once you are all here I shan't interfere, and you will have to do everything yourself—cooking and cleaning and everything."

Peter had never, in her wildest dreams, expected an aunt like this, and for a moment she felt quite shy as she bent forward to kiss her.

"I can't say thank you enough. We'll take care. You'll be surprised how neat and tidy we are. If you can lend me some cleaning and cooking things and some old blankets and cushions for me, I'll tell the others to bring their sleeping-bags. Mine's locked up at Hatchholt, worse luck."

"Very well. Run along now and find your uncle. He'll be with Humphrey in the thirty-acre—I think they're getting it ready for potatoes. You must decide the best way to ask him, but I shouldn't say too much about the *number* of people coming, but concentrate upon getting permission to use the barn . . . Come along . . . I think we had better lock up again . . ."

As she hurried down the cart-track Peter was so excited that she gave little thought to the problem before her.

"It's going to be all right after all," she said to herself as she passed the field she had rolled with Henry before breakfast, and realized that from somewhere ahead was coming a very remarkable noise. First she heard a deep throbbing which she supposed to be a tractor, but this was accompanied by a mournful dirge that could hardly be a human voice. She turned up by the hedge and came to an open gate through which she could see a brown field. On her right it was newly furrowed into the big, deep ridges which, she knew, were ready now to take the potato "seed". Even as she watched, the noise increased as a big red tractor roared over the brow of the hill.

This in itself was an impressive sight, but Peter gasped when she saw her Uncle Micah, with black beard fluttering in the wind, perched on the driving seat. His mouth was open and the frightening accompaniment was Uncle singing hymns! She had never imagined that Uncle Micah would take such a practical part in the running of the farm, and she was even more surprised when he stopped the tractor and glared at her with a very odd expression on his face. "He's baring his teeth at me," Peter thought, and then almost laughed in relief as she realized that this odd grimace was a smile.

"You have sought me out and found me, then, my child?" he rumbled. "What would you have with me?"

Now, as she faced Uncle Micah seated above her on the throbbing tractor, her mind went blank and words failed her. The old man stared at her silently for a moment and then consulted an enormous silver watch.

"You are a good and dutiful daughter to your father, Petronella?"

As this was in the form of a question, Peter gulped and said she tried to be, and this appeared to be the correct answer.

"In ten minutes we will converse again. Tarry here till I return," was the next comment as the tractor roared into life and turned.

So Peter stayed while the tractor disappeared four times over the hill and Uncle Micah changed to a hymn about Jordan. Then he dismounted, put a gnarled hand on her shoulder and led her along the path by the hedge. "You must try not to be lonely here, my child."

And this, of course, was her opportunity, and without really trying to choose her words Peter told him how thrilled and happy she was to be at Seven Gates (a slight exaggeration which seemed justified) and of how she was hoping to show the place to some of her friends from Onnybrook.

"I've been talking to Aunt Carol about it, Uncle, and we thought that if you didn't mind we would ask them over for a day or two . . ."

Then she stole a glance at his face and was shaken by the expression she saw there, but it was too late to stop now.

"Of course, we know there's no room in the house, and it wouldn't be fair to Auntie either. My friends are used to camping and would bring their own food, and we wondered, Uncle, if you'd mind very much if we camped out in . . . in . . . in one of your old barns . . ."

There was an awful silence. Then he muttered, "Nobody *comes* to Seven White Gates. They go. They do not come. It is accursed."

Peter laughed nervously. "I see—— But what a pity, Uncle! I don't think my friends would mind the curse, though. After all, *I've* come, haven't I, and p'raps I've altered it all."

He looked strangely at her, frowned and then said, "Ask your Aunt," and strode moodily back to the tractor. Peter had no idea whether she had got permission or not, and the battle was not finally won until dinner-time, after Uncle Micah had three times forbidden the opening up of the barn.

Aunt Carol won him over eventually when she went out with him into the yard after asking Peter to clear the table.

"I'm afraid we've hurt him rather," she said when she came back. "He says he'll have nothing to do with it or the consequences if we open up the barn, but we'll do it, Peter, and ask your friends. He won't mind when he sees you happy and the others here . . . Now I'll write to Mrs. Morton and you can go down to the post office with the letter right away."

It didn't take long to get down to the village, and the straggling street looked very pleasant in today's sunshine. She felt that she would like to see Jenny again and tell her that the Lone Piners were coming and wondered how she could avoid her inquisitive old parent. If the shop door was open that terrifying bell wouldn't peal! It was, and Peter stepped quietly into the gloom and looked around. In a corner behind the counter by the window sat Jenny. Her red hair was over her eyes, her chin in her hands, and she was bent over a paper-backed book in her lap.

"Hello, Jenny! Where's my bike?"

There was a crash as the chair overturned and Jenny sprawled on the floor.

"Oh! Peter! You are a beast coming in like that all slinky and quiet."

Peter leaned over the counter and whispered: "Can you come out? I've got something special to tell you, and I want to know about my bike."

"I can't come yet. She's out and I'm minding the shop till she comes back . . . But she won't be long, and then I'll come, Peter—I'd love to."

"All right. I say, Jenny. I want some paper and a pen. I've got a special letter to write. Can you lend me some?"

"You'd better come into the office," said Jenny importantly. "And if Mum comes back afore you've done," she went on, "you'd better get down on the floor under the desk and then she won't see you . . . But buck up do, please, Peter, 'cause all this makes me nervous."

Peter found a pen which would write, and then realized that she had a particularly important message to send and that by a later rule of the Lone Pine Club she ought to write in code. She had just closed the envelope and was drawing the silhouette of the Lonely Pine on the flap when she heard the sound of singing in the street. Somehow the voice seemed familiar, and when, with it, came the steady "clip-clop" of a horse's hooves, she rushed out to join Jenny on the pavement, and there was Reuben on the driving seat of the caravan, with Miranda at his side!

"Hello!" Peter called excitedly. "Hello, Mr. Reuben! It's me, Peter! I got here safely! Where are you going?"

The gipsy woman smiled a welcome.

"So you are safe and well, eh? That's good. And the old man?" asked Reuben.

"Yes! Yes!" she said. "He's all right, too, thank you. . . . At least I *suppose* he is really . . . He's a bit peculiar."

The gipsy smiled again.

"Maybe. We are going to Onnybrook round the side of the mountain. We are told we shall sell baskets there . . . We do not like this place, but we said we would pass your farm again to see if there was anything we might do for you . . ."

Peter was so excited that she did not see an ominous figure hurrying up the pavement towards them.

"Could you go to Witchend, Mr. Reuben? *Please* would you do that for me? I've got two letters, and if you could take them it would be much better and safer—and more mysterious, too," she added half to herself.

He grinned and touched his old hat.

"Deliver tomorrow, missy. Safer than postman," and he leaned down to take the two letters. Before Peter could pass them up an acid voice at her side said:

"Come inside this very minute, Jenny! How dare you stand there talking to idle, good-for-nothing vagabonds! . . . And as for you, miss," she added, turning to Peter, "I'll trouble you not to come seeking my girl again. We want nothing here from Seven Gates."

And with this parting shot Mrs. Harman flourished her umbrella and stumped into her own shop and set the bell a-jangling.

Jenny, following reluctantly, turned with a wink and hissed: "Meet you outside the garage in a tick."

The two gipsies looked at each other and then at Peter.

"You hear what she called us?" Miranda said at last.

"'Tis no matter. Come, Miss Petronella. Give me the letters, for we have far to go."

Before giving Reuben the letters Peter opened the one for David and hastily scribbled another few lines.

"Thank you, Mr. Reuben. And you will truly deliver them tomorrow? You know Witchend, don't you? Up the road from Onnybrook Station and then to the right at the top of the hill . . ."

As she spoke she felt a tug at her shorts and saw the brown-faced gipsy child beside her.

"Hallo, Fenella! Been driving the caravan by yourself, lately?"

The child shook her head and shyly held up something in a grubby hand.

"Take it, if you please, little lady," Miranda smiled. "She has made it for you. Try it! It is a true Romany whistle. Nobody else can make like it. Keep it, and when you whistle on it the Romany will come to you if they can hear."

Wonderingly, Peter put the beautifully carved little toy to her lips and blew. The sound was soft, sweet, yet piercing, and the piebald between the shafts put her ears forward at the sound. Reuben laughed.

"Keep it always, little *chi*. It is the Romany's gift to you. Now we must go, for we must be over the mountain by nightfall . . . but we'll meet again, and we will tell your friends that all is well with you," and he clucked his tongue to the horse and Fenella ran around as the caravan started and clambered up the steps.

Peter stood for a moment with her hand raised in farewell and then looked round for the garage. She saw two old petrol pumps much in need of a coat of paint farther up the street and strolled towards them. An old man in faded dungarees came out into the sunshine, leaned against the yellow pump and produced a fragment of cigarette from behind his ear.

"Is my bicycle ready?" Peter asked. "Jenny Harman left it. It had a puncture."

"Aye," the man said, gesturing into the gloomy depths behind him.

Peter wandered in and found her bicycle mixed up with several others in course of repair.

"Thank you," she said. "How much is that?"

"Nine," said the man tersely, and after Peter had paid that was all there was to it.

Jenny came out of the post office. "Come *on*, Peter," she hissed dramatically; "I've run away again. Let's go exploring, and then you can tell me the secret you promised."

"But you can't keep on running away from home like this," Peter protested.

"Oh, I always run away," Jenny explained. "I always have and I always shall. You see, she's not my *real* mother. I haven't got a real one . . . This one is a step, and now

Daddy's in the army and I hate it. But I never take much notice of her when she's beastly like she is now . . . and most particularly I want to be your friend, Peter . . ."

"All right then, Jenny. Let's be friends. Will you come to tea now at Seven Gates?"

The other girl hesitated.

"It's nice of you, Peter, but . . . but I don't think I will . . . not today, but perhaps some other time when . . . when I feel more like it . . ." she finished rather lamely.

Peter felt rather hurt.

"All right, then. Where shall we go? Are you going to fetch your bike?"

"No. But you bring yours and leave it by the first white gate and I'll take you up Black Dingle."

So the two girls trudged back up the hill again and, just as they had done the night before, turned up the second lane. Jenny had lived all her life in Barton Beach and was thrilled with all that Peter could tell her of school life and of her life at Hatchholt and of her friends the Mortons.

"And we've asked them to come to Seven Gates for a few days, Jenny. When we explore the mountain you'd better come and be our guide. I suppose you'd have to run away from home every day, but you don't seem to mind that!"

"I'd love that, Peter! I've never had friends like you have and we could have lots of fun."

Then, as they followed the lane still uphill, Jenny began to tell Peter all sorts of odd and inconsequent stories about the Stiperstones. She told how the Romans had mined all this strange, wild country for lead and the hills around had, until only a few years ago, been worked and quarried.

"But I've had an adventure, Peter. An *awful adventure*, and that's why I've brought you up this way. I'll tell you about it when we get to the place. Look! This is Black Dingle."

Peter looked round with interest. Ever since they had left the wood and the first white gate, they had been climbing. Now there were loose stones underfoot, and the road was now but a rough track. They had reached a little plateau at the foot of a rocky gorge which cut up into the side of the mountain on their right. A grey old signpost with one weather-beaten arm pointing up the valley road, read "Black Dingle to Devil's Chair".

There was something eerie and frightening about this place. Suddenly she knew why the gipsies shunned it and said it was evil. She looked and saw the big, black mass of the Devil's Chair athwart the skyline six hundred feet above her, and realized why those who lived in its shadow felt there was something wicked about it. Then she looked up the Dingle and saw that, unlike the lovely green turf and bracken of Hatchholt, this track was wild and rough, and that even the stream which crossed the little plateau a few yards in front of her ran black and sullen. She shivered a little and turned to Jenny as a mournful whistle broke the silence.

"P'raps we oughtn't to go any farther," Jenny said. "P'raps that was one of the Whistlers. I've never exactly heard them, but maybe that's one."

"What do you mean, Jenny? What Whistlers?"

"Why, the Seven Whistlers, of course. Haven't you ever heard of them?"

Peter shook her head.

"No, I haven't, and you can tell me about them as we climb—and about your great adventure, too. I didn't come all the way up here just to look at this silly old signpost, but to explore, and I'm jolly well going to do it . . . Come on, Jenny! Don't be stupid. Come and lead the way and then when the others come we shall know where to take them . . . Now tell me about the Whistlers . . ."

Jenny gulped and turned up the track.

"All right then. I don't care really and I'll tell you my adventure too. I remember Dad telling me once that the Whistlers are seven mysterious birds sometimes heard whistling all together at night. When you hear them in the night like that it's bad, and the miners round here often wouldn't go to work because an accident might happen to them . . . it's horrid. I hate them."

"Well, you needn't worry about *that* whistle," said the practical Peter, "because it was a curlew. We have them at home and it's no use trying to frighten me with *them*. Now tell me of your adventure."

"P'raps I don't want to tell you now," replied the aggrieved Jenny. "What's the sense if you don't believe me before I start? I believe you're laughing at me."

"No, I'm not laughing at you, Jenny. Let's climb as far as we can first, and then you tell me your story."

So they followed the track which crossed and recrossed the little stream, but the valley did not change its character much. The sides of the gorge on their right were almost precipitous, and although the lower slopes were covered sparsely with heather and a few stunted hawthorns, the ground was too rocky for turf or flowers. As they climbed, the Dingle widened, and the cliff face on the left, although very high, seemed strangely pitted and marked.

Peter asked the meaning.

"Those are the entrances to the old mines, I believe," said Jenny. "Or they are caves. I'm not sure which. Dad told me that just before I was born those mines over there were worked, but I've never been up to explore. Shall we go one day? There's some of the old miners' cottages at the foot of the cliff—they're all in ruins now and full of bit-bats and owls . . . But it's just about here that my adventure began. Would you like to hear it now?"

Peter agreed that she would, and listened attentively.

"Well, Peter," Jenny was saying. "I hadn't been up here for ages, but one afternoon 'bout six weeks ago, when it got dark early, I came with George Campling, who said he knew of a magpie's nest. We came up this way and then he couldn't find the tree and we forgot the time and almost before we knew, it was getting dark . . . Now, Peter, what I'm going to tell is true 'cos we *know* about the Black Riders. If you know history you know about Wild Edric and Godda. And you know too that Edric is buried under this mountain waiting for the world's end, but sometimes he hunts at night, and if you see him then something awful happens . . ."

Jenny's voice died away and Peter turned to look at her. She was *really* frightened! Her face, with its halo of red hair and its big freckles, was very white and she passed her tongue over her lips while Peter slipped an arm through hers and said gently enough:

"Go on, Jenny. I'm not laughing at you."

Suddenly Peter remembered what old Henry had told her this very morning about a girl in Barton Beach who had seen the ghostly hunt.

"Jenny!" she gasped. "You didn't *see* the Riders, did you? You weren't the girl who saw them, were you?"

Jenny nodded. "I was . . . Oh! Peter. I've been scared to come here again and I thought if I came with you I'd be brave because you're so brave. But I'm not feeling very brave and it was about here it happened."

They had come now to the widest part of the valley. Ahead of them the Chair still loomed terrific over the head of the gorge and it was difficult to see how the track found its way up to the summit. Three hawthorns, their gnarled trunks white with sheep's wool, and two big boulders marked where their track divided with the left-hand fork leading over towards the old mines.

"We stopped here a bit," Jenny continued hurriedly, "to look in those trees and then, very quickly, it seemed to get dark and I said we'd better run for it 'cause if we didn't hurry it would be quite dark before we got home. And George said, 'Right-o,' and a cloud came up and we couldn't see much and suddenly . . . and *suddenly*, Peter, we heard horses galloping. 'Twas faint and far away, but we knew it was the Black Hunt. We ran home hard as we could and even as we ran we could hear those horses coming after us—sometimes quite close and sometimes far away. But it was them, Peter. I know it was, although I didn't actually see them and neither did George, *but it was them* and I'll tell you how I know. The Black Riders always come before something awful happens. Dad says they rode up here before the last war and this one too. And this time when we got home at last and George told someone, we began to wonder a bit, but next day old Humphrey up at your farm heard that his boy was a prisoner in Germany, so you see how right it is."

"Is it?" said Peter. "*He* didn't hear the ghost hunt or see it either, did he?"

"No, he didn't," Jenny replied, "that's true enough. But somebody else saw them afore Dunkirk too, so you can't help believing, can you?"

Peter was not very impressed. She wanted, now that she had got so far, to climb to the top and suggested it to her new friend.

But Jenny would not agree to this.

"No," she said. "No, Peter. I'm sorry, but I won't go to the Chair."

Then she pointed dramatically upwards.

"*Peter*," she whispered. "*Look! It's going. It's the mist. He's coming to his throne.* Quick! We must run," and at this, she grabbed Peter's hand and dragged her back down the way they had come.

Peter knew how the mountain mist came suddenly like this to these hills and valleys. Once she had been caught in just such a mist with her father, and last summer, of course, the twins had been lost too. Even as she looked back, the hard outline of the Chair wavered and disappeared. Then the atmosphere became cold and clammy as the fog swirled round them. Suddenly Jenny gave a stifled little scream and pointed up the track which led to the mines. Shadowy in the thickening mist, the two girls seemed to see a figure on horseback waving ghostly arms but no sound of hooves came to their straining ears. Then, far away on the hilltop, it seemed to Peter that tiny, gnome-like figures flitted in uncanny procession.

Jenny turned and wailed into Peter's shoulder.

"Peter. It's true. It's them. They're riding again. What

shall we do, Peter? We must hide our eyes. We mustn't even see them. *Don't look, Peter.*"

Even Peter wavered a moment at this outburst, but before she could recover herself, a new sound came to them through the mist. Somewhere from over their heads, the silence was broken by a weird, throbbing hum. The thickening air vibrated as the sound increased and, as Jenny cowered in terror at her feet, Peter, looking up, saw a gigantic black, shadowy bulk rushing over their heads.

4. The Lone Piners Join Up

THREE DAYS after Peter had made her adventurous journey to Seven Gates, her friends, only a few miles away, were wishing she was with them, as they toiled slowly up towards the famous Lone Pine Camp for the first meeting of the Club since the Christmas holidays.

There were four in the party. First came David, nearly sixteen now, wearing jeans and a sweater and carrying a laden haversack. He tramped on steadily without taking any notice of the petulant duet behind him, as the twins, Richard and Mary, rather breathless and hand in hand, strove desperately to keep up with his long strides. They were absurdly alike, and today both were wearing blue shorts, yellow shirts, grey socks and brown anoraks. Perhaps it was Mary's curls that made her seem to be a fraction taller than her twin.

The fourth member was a black Scottie dog called Macbeth, whose affection for Mary was only equalled by Mary's loyalty to her twin.

"I don't suppose you're really interested to know what *we* think . . ." Dickie was saying as David jumped a stream without even looking back at them.

"'Course he's not interested," Mary continued. "'Course he isn't. He's just a selfish old beast hidin' the letter and not letting us see."

"It's always the same, twin," complained Dickie. "No 'sideration for others . . . David! Why do you go so fast? You know Mary and me can't cross this foamin' torrent without a . . . a . . . a canoe or something."

"I know why it is, Dickie. He's afraid we'll see what Peter's written."

"Yes. He just thinks she's *his* friend."

"I know. His little girl friend, Dickie. That's what he thinks." Then in a wheedling, sweet-as-sugar-candy little voice, "David dear. PLEASE let us see Peter's letter NOW. We're tired out, David dear, you makin' us hurry like this."

"It's all we ask," her twin went on. "Jus' a silly little thing like seeing a letter. Nothin' difficult like making the sweet ration go round, f'rinstance. Jus' reading a letter and findin' out when she's coming . . ."

"Silly, I call it . . ."

"*We* call it, twin. Jus' silly . . . an' selfish, of course." David turned round.

"If you didn't talk so much, Dickie, you'd remember your jobs. Now you'll have to go back to the stream and fill the kettle. And then you'll both have to find some twigs to start the fire—there will be plenty at this time of year just inside the wood. And before you go back, Dickie, I'll tell you once and for all that I'm not going to open the letter until we're in the camp and Tom is with us. You're both little nuisances today, so buck up and get some wood and some water and we'll open up camp . . . And why are you so impatient, anyway? It doesn't *matter*, does it, when you hear what Peter has to say?"

Mary looked at her twin and they both grinned before turning back together to the stream to fill the kettle.

The Lone Pine Camp which Mary and Peter had found last summer was a lovely little hollow of green turf hidden by gorse and brambles at the top of the wild hillside of the Witchend valley. One solitary great pine tree stood as a sentinel in the centre of the clearing, and, from even its lowest branches, a look-out could see down into Witchend itself, across the dense wood below, right up the lonely winding valley to the tableland of the Long Mynd. Apart from a narrow tunnel under the gorse, through which only the twins could squeeze, there was but one entrance to the camp, and now, as David pushed his way through the brambles which seemed to have grown since the Christmas holidays, Dickie said:

"Gosh! I hope nobody has found it while we've been away."

All was well. There were no signs of enemy occupation —no scraps of paper, empty tins or cigarette ends. The stones of the fireplace were still in position and the framework of the shelter, which in the summer was covered with bracken, was still intact.

"Put down the kettle, kids," he said, "and run off for some kindling. Bring some fir cones, too, and we'll soon have the fire going."

While they were away David took out his clasp-knife and prised up a square of turf between the roots of the pine tree, and disclosed a rusty old tin. In this were kept the secret documents of the Lone Pine Club—the rules, the log-book and the signatures in blood made by the original members last summer. Then he sat back on his heels and pulled from his jacket the note which Peter had scribbled in the wood by the Minsterly road.

They soon got the fire burning, and while Dickie was hoisted into the crow's nest in the tree, Mary unpacked the haversack. But Tom Ingles must have been learning some woodcraft, for not even the sentry's sharp eyes spotted him as he came through the wood, and it was Macbeth who put his head on one side and whined as, clear and loud, through the stillness of the afternoon, came the mournful cry of the peewit. This was the secret warning signal of the Lone Piners which Tom had taught them all last summer.

David looked up from the fire and Macbeth barked and wagged his tail—he knew this whistle—as Dickie scrambled to the ground and ran out to meet their friend.

Tom Ingles, although only a few weeks younger than David, was smaller and slighter. His friendship for the Mortons and Peter was the best thing that had happened to him, and although he pretended sometimes that the Club was "all right just for the kids," he was secretly very proud of his membership.

"Hello, David. Hello, Mary. How's things?" he said, as

he came into the clearing. "Did you hear me call and have you heard from Peter? I came as soon as I could, but Uncle's always finding me something to do . . . Oh, sorry, Mackie! Didn't I speak to you . . . ?"

Then they all sat down round the fire and David balanced the kettle across the two stones of the fireplace before taking out Peter's letter again.

"It came this morning," he said, "but I thought we'd read it together."

When he had finished it—and it didn't take long—they all began to speak together.

"Poor old Peter," said David. "How beastly for her not to like where she's going."

"I tell you *what*," was Dickie's contribution. "We'll all jolly well go and rescue her. Let's start now. Bet she's afraid of those old Stiperstones . . ."

"She said to warn me," said Tom. "Wonder what she meant?"

"She says she's going to send us another message and we've got to be ready," Mary broke in. "That's the important thing for us . . . Now you see, David, why we wanted to see that letter earlier. We guessed she'd want us to help, didn't we, twin?"

David tied up the muslin bag containing the tea and dropped it into the kettle of boiling water.

Then they ate their cakes and sandwiches and Tom took some potatoes out of his pocket and poked them into the embers. But it was a gloomy meal and not at all like the jolly feasts of the summer, or indeed like the one or two hurried snacks round the fire which they had enjoyed last holidays, when the gorse had been little protection from the wind and the frost had crackled underfoot and the short day was nearly over at four o'clock.

David poured them all some tea.

"Of course I know we all ought to go and see her and cheer her up if we can, but it's too far for the twins to go there and back in a day even on bikes. And you know, too, that Mother wouldn't let us go off on an expedition like that unless we had an invitation."

"Well, we got that," Dickie broke in. "Peter practically invites us herself."

"And if she doesn't say that," Mary went on, "well, then we'll invite us. I will. Now . . ."

"Don't be crazy, twins," David said soberly. "You know jolly well that we'll have to have a proper invitation from her aunt before we could ask to go. Surely you see that?"

"Well," said Mary, "it's always us gets the ideas. Now I've got one. Let's cycle over and ask for an invitation. It's easy . . ."

"It's always easy when we do it!" finished Dickie triumphantly.

But David was still puzzled and turned to Tom.

"There's something odd about all this, Tom. I told you old Mr. Sterling came over to see us in his best suit and a funny-looking bowler hat, and told us he was going to Birmingham for a bit. I couldn't understand then why he wouldn't let Peter stay with us. He didn't answer when Mother asked him, but of course he was nice enough and very polite, and he raised his hat lots of times between the door and the gate . . . I don't see that we can do anything more until we get this special message she talks about . . . Now just before we all sign the book and get these things washed up you'd better nip up into the look-out, Mary, and see if there's anything happening."

So, rather reluctantly, Mary put her foot in the rope stirrup which always hung from the lowest branch of the tree and hauled herself up.

"Guess we won't wash up till tomorrow," Dickie murmured as he turned Macbeth over on his back and tickled his chest. "Or maybe David could carry the dirty things down in the haversack to old Agnes and ask her to wash up."

Before David could make a suitable reply an excited squeak from Mary brought him to his feet.

"Come up here, Dickie! Come quickly. There's something *most* mysterious comin' down the lane—it's not a car and it's not any one of Mr. Ingles's wagons—at least I don't think it is . . . I saw it turn out of the Onnybrook road into the lane—NO. NOT YOU, DAVID! IT'S DICKIE I WANT!"

So David shrugged and helped his brother up into the tree. Then there was a long silence until the twins said together:

"All right, David. You'd better come too . . . And Tom."

Swaying down the lane, gleaming cheerfully in the pale afternoon sun, came a gay caravan.

"Gosh!" breathed Dickie. "The chimney's smokin'!"

"It's stopped at Ingles. Stop hopping about, Dickie, else I can't see."

"That's a women with something bright round her head and carrying a bundle going through the gate . . . Here! Come on, Mary—please let us down, David. We're in a hurry."

But David didn't move.

"You needn't think you're going down to Ingles till we've all signed the book and the crocks have been washed up. If Peter was here I know she'd insist."

The twins looked at each other, and then Mary said sweetly enough:

"Very well, David, just as you say. Let's hurry up and get the chores done, and then we can go and see the caravan."

So David and the twins came down, leaving Tom to watch and report.

"She's at the back door now . . . Auntie is talking to her . . . Bet you she gets her a cup of tea . . . Now there's a kid got out of the caravan. She's swinging on the gate. She'll catch it if Uncle sees her."

Suddenly there was a shout from David.

"Come here, you two! Come back and do your jobs."

Two muffled voices came from the other side of the gorse.

"'Bye, David dear. 'Bye, Tom."

"Be good little boys and wash up nicely. Come on, Mackie," and the voices died away down the hillside.

"Did they catch you, David?" Tom called down.

"They did," said David ruefully. "I ought to have known when Mary agreed to do the chores. Silly of me . . . you see, they know what to do together sometimes without talking about it at all . . ."

"How did they get out?"

"When I wasn't looking they crawled through that narrow tunnel in the gorse. What's the caravan doing now, Tom? Just give me a hand and I'll come up again."

"It looks as if Auntie is buying something, and I'm sure she's brought out a cup of tea . . . Look! There are those two just jumping the stream."

And so they were. Breathlessly the twins raced down the narrow path which followed the tinkling stream down the valley. Soon they came to Witchend itself, tucked snugly against the hillside. They climbed to the top of the fence which was supposed to keep the heather from their garden and waited for Macbeth, who was yelping after a rabbit.

"If we really hurry now, Mary, we might catch it before he turns round and goes back. Gosh! But I'd like to know what it's like inside and what that woman is selling and if she's got any charms . . ."

"Yes, I know," Mary interrupted. "Spells and things. Frog's legs."

"It's only witches have those."

"Well," panted his twin triumphantly, "p'raps she's a witch."

And then quite suddenly they were face to face with her, for they turned a corner in the lane and the red and yellow caravan filled the road in front of them.

From the driving seat the gipsy woman, with a scarlet handkerchief round her black hair, smiled with a flash of white teeth. At her side sat a solemn little girl, and from somewhere out of sight came the sound of a man singing.

The horse stopped and the twins stood hand in hand in the middle of the road.

"Good afternoon," said Mary politely. Then: "This road doesn't lead anywhere, you know."

"If you'll excuse us mentioning it," added Dickie.

Then a voice from the back called: "What is it, *romni*? Drive on!"

The woman shook her ear-rings. "Once this road led to Witchend. Doesn't it now?"

Mary almost stuttered in her excitement.

"Do you really mean you were coming to Witchend?"

"Specially to see *us*?" added Dickie.

But before the woman could answer, a gipsy man, with even bigger ear-rings, came round from behind the van. He smiled, too, and looked them up and down in a way which was quite familiar to them.

"Yes," said Mary. "We're twins. I'm Mary Morton and this is Dickie."

"We're alike," added her brother. Then, "Are you really coming to see us?"

Reuben nodded.

"If we may," he said, "we come to Witchend. We have a message for Mr. David Morton. Is he here?"

"Not exactly *there*," said Dickie, "but he's just our brother, and we'll take the message. Is it a letter?"

Reuben tapped his heart.

"It is a letter from a lady," he smiled. "And we must deliver it to him. Also there is a letter for Mrs. Morton. . . . Shall we go?"

"What I'd like to know," Mary said slowly, "is how you've got a letter from a lady for David. Who is it and who are you?"

"Come back with us," the woman said, "and you will know all. Climb up here with Fenella, my lucky ones, and drive us in. It is lucky to drive a Romany van . . . But wait till I am down."

The twins scrambled up and without a word the gipsy child moved over and handed the reins to Dickie, who passed one to Mary. Then Reuben went to the horse's head and clicked his tongue and the caravan lurched up the lane.

"Dickie," whispered Mary, "you know who the letter's from, don't you? *It's the message from Peter.* She said wait for a message, didn't she? Well, here it is."

The sound of rumbling wheels, a man's voice singing and a cheerful chatter in which she seemed to recognize something of her own brought Mrs. Morton over to the gate in time to see the caravan turn the last corner of the lane.

Reuben stepped forward and removed his battered old hat. "We have a message for you, *rawni*—a message from over the evil mountain, and a letter, too, for Mr. David Morton. Is he here yet?"

And then Miranda took up the tale of how they had met the twins in the lane, and finished by saying:

"We have come far, and if it please you we would camp here for the night and be away early in the morning. Perhaps the *rawni* needs baskets . . . We have plenty to show."

"Camp here?" Mary called down ecstatically. "Camp at Witchend? Oh, Mummy! Do please let them stay . . . Oh! *please* do—and let them make a fire and sing round it."

Reuben smiled at Mrs. Morton.

"We will not sing, but we would like to stay. Trust us, lady, and by your door in the morning will be wood cut ready and another offering from the Romany."

Mrs. Morton looked at them both and then at Fenella up aloft, and when the child smiled shyly at her she nodded.

"Of course you can stay. I'm alone here except for a housekeeper, but you're welcome. Open the gate and come in, and may I have my letter, please?"

So as the twins came home in state Reuben passed over two envelopes, and when Mrs. Morton saw David's she laughed and said:

"I know who that's from! Dickie . . . you'd better run and fetch David—and Tom, too, if he's there. Tell David I've got a very important letter for him . . . No, Mary, you stay here with me."

Reuben looked round, selected the best place for his camp, and then released his horse and turned him off on to the hillside. Miranda busied herself inside the caravan and eventually invited Mary to inspect their home, but before she could see much there was a cheerful shout from outside and Dickie called triumphantly:

"Here they are. I met them coming down. Hurry up, David, and get your message. *We* know who it's from and you'd better jolly well buck up and tell us what is in it."

David took the letter from his mother, while Tom watched the gipsies with deep suspicion.

"They're up to no good, I'll be bound," he muttered. "I wonder Uncle didn't send them packing. What is it, David. What's all the fuss about?"

"It's another note from Peter. The gipsies brought it. Call the kids and we'll go over there where the others can't hear us."

And when the twins were balanced precariously on the top bar of the gate looking over David's shoulder the envelope bearing the familiar silhouette of the Lone Pine was opened. On a sheet of paper torn from a common pad was an unintelligible jumble of words. There was no address and no date, and this is what they read:

"SAUCEPANS AND ALL EGGS AND LONE EVERY DAY PINERS MUST EXCEL COME YESTERDAY THEN SEVEN EIGHT MARJORIE GATES TOO MUST TO AFTER ALL STAY AND THEN FOR HIS FIRST WEEK DON'T GUESS EVERYTHING BUT SEE ARRANGED AND THEN ASK UNCLE JACK YOUR OF THE MOTHER MUST BE COME WITH US ON BETTER NOT BIKES AND BETTER BETTER THEN TO BRING THEODORE OLIVER SALLY ALSO COMES AS EVERYONE MUST PACK FOR EVERY HORSE ANOTHER DAYS GREAT AHEAD OF SURPRISE FOR YOU FOR KENNETH AND YOU BECAUSE SEEN EVERYTHING MUST BE ALL ON THE RIGHT

LINES BEFORE NOW BUT CHARLES BUT AGAIN THEN SOME
HAVE SOLVED MYSTERY EVEN IF BEARER FORGETS WHICH
OF THEN ALL THIS TANK BUSTER CAN ALWAYS HOPE BE
SITTING UP TRUSTED OVER HEADS PETER AGAIN THEN P.S.
ALWAYS INTERRUPTED BETTER EVEN TO COME THEN NEXT
DAY BEFORE WE AFTER EVEN COMING RECEIVING WITHOUT
DOUBT THIS OLD FAITHFUL REUBEN MUST AND WILL NEVER
OVERLOOK TELL SO MANY YOU STILL HOPE BEST OLD
METHOD WAY TO ALWAYS BRING AWAKE OR SLEEPING EVEN
RICHARD BAGS TRUNKS BAGS AND WHEN SCOUTS CAMPING
BEFORE THEY GEAR."

They looked at it in horror.

"Gosh!" said Tom with a whistle. "Poor kid! She's
gone crackers. Just look at it! Why—it's not even sense."

"Silly, I call it," was Mary's comment. "Why does she
do it like that, David? . . . You're her special friend. You
tell us."

Then Dickie fell off the gate in excitement, and because
no one seemed to notice it he was furious.

"You silly, selfish old beasts, all of you . . . An' stupid,
too. Yes, silly! You think you know everything, but you
don't . . . And you didn't even notice when I fell off here
and jolly nearly killed myself . . . 'Course I know *you're*
sorry, Mary, aren't you?"

Mary nodded and slipped off the gate. Dickie whispered
to her, and then they strolled over towards the caravan.

"Blowed if I know what to make of it, Tom," David
said ruefully. "It's silly, and of course it's from Peter, but
what she's up to I don't know."

Tom took it out of his hand. "It's a code, I expect,"
he said. "But we haven't got one, have we? We talked
of it once, I know, but never fixed it . . . What's the matter
with those kids? They're giggling as if they *knew* something.
Hi! Dickie! Come here."

The twins strolled over casually.

"Acksherly," said Dickie proudly, "we know all about
this message. *You* don't know, but *we* know. Acksherly,

Peter must have meant it for us, but just put the name on the envelope wrong."

"Yes," said Mary. "An' it's a pity you don't take more notice of us, 'cause when you don't you always get in a muddle. Shall *we* tell them, twin?" she added hurriedly, as she noticed Tom's furious face.

Then Dickie looked at his brother and decided.

"Peter and me made it up one wet afternoon at Christmas. You'd all gone for a walk, but we had colds when she was staying here. We forgot to tell you, I s'pose . . . ALL RIGHT, DAVID. I'M TELLING YOU, AREN'T I? . . . ALL RIGHT. Well—it's every third word makes the message. Try it."

So they rushed in for a pencil and wrote out the proper message, which read:

"ALL LONE PINERS COME SEVEN GATES TO STAY FOR WEEK EVERYTHING ARRANGED ASK YOUR MOTHER COME ON BIKES BETTER BRING SALLY AS PACK HORSE GREAT SURPRISE FOR YOU EVERYTHING ALL RIGHT NOW BUT SOME MYSTERY BEARER OF THIS CAN BE TRUSTED PETER P.S. BETTER COME DAY AFTER RECEIVING THIS REUBEN WILL TELL YOU BEST WAY BRING SLEEPING BAGS AND CAMPING GEAR."

When David had written down the last word, he said, "Good old Peter! Isn't she grand, Tom? What a rag if we can fix it. She says ask Mother, so we'd better see if she's got a message, too."

And Mrs. Morton's message was just as exciting, but she refused to talk until the twins were quiet. Then: "Yes, I know all about it, and I don't see why it can't be managed. I've got an invitation for you all here to go and stay with Peter's aunt, Mrs. Caroline Sterling, at Seven Gates. She doesn't say very much, and I must say I think it heroic of her to take you all on, but it's a charming letter, and if you want to go you can . . . Now can you tell me what Peter says? It was from Peter, wasn't it?"

So David told her all he could, and together they puzzled over the sleeping-bag and camping gear until

Mrs. Morton forced from them a reluctant promise that they wouldn't camp out of doors until the weather was better. "NOT the twins, anyhow," she compromised at last.

Poor Tom looked rather rueful.

"I reckon Uncle won't let me go," he said. "Don't see how he could, anyway for a day or two, but I'll come up in the morning and let you know . . . Anyway, Peter seems more cheerful than she was in the other letter. Reckon I'd like to know what's happened."

Then Mrs. Morton and old Agnes, the housekeeper, began to fuss about packing and the twins' bedtime, but in between all the commotion David and Tom managed to slip out and talk to the friendly gipsies. David asked them how they had met Peter, and Reuben told them.

Then Tom went home to Ingles and David ran in to tell his mother about Peter, but all she said when she heard the story was:

"It's just what I would have expected of her, David. Bless her!"

Then the twins were packed off to bed protesting, and after supper David wandered over to the caravan. The gipsies asked him in, and he shared a seat on one of the bunks and drank tea out of a chipped mug, while Reuben told him the best way to Seven Gates.

"You'd best go right over the top, young man; it's the quickest in the end. Go round this mountain by Onny-brook road and then head straight for Stiperstones and then up to Devil's Chair. When you're up seek for a steep valley on your left called Black Dingle, and that will take you down to Seven Gates."

But when David questioned him about Peter's mysterious relations and the farm, neither of them would say much and they changed the subject.

"But it's a strange country, Mr. David, as I was telling your friend. A strange, wild country and a bad country, too. But over other side of Stiperstones there's places full of old Roman mines, they say. And you'll take care with those little 'uns when you're on the hills, for the rocks and stones are loose and there's many an old mine shaft has fallen in and many a quarry long since forgotten."

Suddenly there was a fumbling at the door of the caravan and an urgent, tragic voice whispered: "David! Are you in there? Let me in!"

Reuben opened the door. Below, at the foot of the steps, stood the twins. Their faces looked white in the light from the hanging lamp, and as they were both only in pyjamas and dressing-gowns, their teeth were chattering with the cold.

"What's the matter?" David demanded.

"Oh, don't make a fuss for a minute, David," Mary said as she climbed up into the warmth. "Just close the door while we tell you the awfullest news."

"G-g-g-o-sh! David!" stuttered the shivering Dickie. "Oh, gosh, David! It's the worst news I ever knew . . . I guess it's fatal," he added inconsequently.

"All right, David," Mary broke in. "Mummy and Agnes are in the kitchen doin' things, and they don't know we're here. We want you to go and tell her to stop packing and things like that."

"You see, David," Dickie went on, "Mummy's just wastin' her time. Just fritterin' it away, as Agnes says."

David and the gipsies stared at them in bewilderment, and even Fenella sat up in the top bunk and rubbed her eyes.

"What are you burbling about?" said David angrily. "Stop being little idiots and get back to bed."

Mary's eyes were enormous in her pale face.

"David," she said tragically, "*we can't go*. Well, *I* can't, anyway. I don't know about Dickie, but I don't think he can go either . . . he'd better not, anyway."

Her twin looked uneasy at this remark, but repeated almost as if hypnotised:

"No, we can't go."

Suddenly Mary's eyes filled with tears and she choked a little as she said:

"It's Mackie, David. Nobody's thought about him. He hasn't got a bicycle and he can't go all that way running on his legs. They're too little and stumpy. You know they are, David . . . Nobody thinks about him 'cept me, and now he can't go, so I can't go, so Dickie can't go, and you'd better go an' tell Mummy you're going by yourself."

And then, quite unexpectedly, she sobbed and held out her hand in the optimistic hope that her twin would have a handkerchief. He had not, so David passed over his.

David explained the dilemma as best he could to their bewildered new friends. Then Reuben laughed and said something quietly to his wife, who picked up the beginnings of a basket from the floor and went over to Mary.

"Look, little *chi*! Your dog shall go with you tomorrow. Tonight, while you sleep, we will finish making this, which will be his carriage, and he can ride in it on the back of your bicycle. All will be ready in the morning."

The twins were really awed by this generosity and for once could say little more than grateful "thank yous" before they said "Good night" as David opened the door of the caravan.

The night was clear. High up to their left towered the tapering treetops of the Witchend wood, and over behind the darkened house rose the steep curves of the Long Mynd. The little stream, ice-cold from the bogs at the top of the mountain, chattered away at their feet, and far away a fox barked as David opened the door of the house quietly and gave the twins a gentle push up the stairs.

Then he went in to find his mother and thank her for the fun they were sure to have tomorrow.

5. Pilgrims' Progress

DAVID shared a bedroom with Dickie at Witchend. It was a room with a long sloping floor and a little dormer window looking out over the stream to the edge of the wood. Since the very first night he had pushed his bed right under the window, so that he had seemed to be sleeping almost on the mountain itself.

On the morning after Peter's note had been brought by the gipsies, he woke early. He groped for his watch. Ten minutes past six. He slipped out of the bedclothes and leaned from the window.

Outside, the mist hung heavily in the valley and drops of moisture were falling from the eaves. The treetops rose oddly out of the grey sea, like stumpy spears, and, down below, the bulk of the caravan loomed grotesquely. Then a soft voice called: "Ah! you wake at last, then? Already I throw three pebbles and here is the fourth in my hand!"

David looked down to see Reuben laughing up at him.

"Thanks, Reuben," he said. "I'd forgotten I asked you to wake me. Hope you haven't cracked the window."

"Come out quietly, then, and take some tea with us," said the gipsy. "We must be off soon, for the day will be hot and we have far to go on the Ludlow road."

So David washed and dressed and slipped quietly out of the front door. Over by the caravan a wood fire crackled and burned up brightly, and Miranda stirred something in the black pot. She looked up as David came towards her through the wet grass and smiled a welcome.

Reuben came down the steps of the van with a teapot and three mugs in his hand. He jerked his head in the direction of the caravan roof at David's questioning glance, and the latter saw then that the stove inside was alight and the chimney smoking. He leaned against a wheel and cupped his cold hands round the mug, while the gipsies sipped their tea as if it was only lukewarm.

"You will tell the pretty Petronella that the Romany kept their word," Miranda said, and when David nodded, "Of course," she went on—"Tell her from us to keep away from the top of the mountain over there and wish her luck for us . . . And when we have gone wish good luck also to your lady-mother for her hospitality . . . Ask her, if you please, to take this gift from her Romany friends."

And here Reuben reached up into the van and brought out two baskets.

"This for the lady," he said, "and this one for the little dog. It will fix on the bicycle and he will travel all the way."

David thanked him and listened as Reuben went over their route again.

"It's your quickest way to go straight for the mountain and then down the Dingle. At the foot of the hill this side as you come to it, you will find an inn called 'Hope Anchor.' Bide there awhile afore you climb up and if weather looks bad and you cannot see the rocks of the Chair—well bide where you are and don't go up. If 'tis fine and clear you will soon be up and over . . ."

Just then there was a frantic barking and Dickie, Mary and Macbeth erupted from the front door.

David put down his mug hurriedly. He knew what was going to happen and was wondering what he was going to say. The twins had blue raincoats on over their pyjamas. Mary was stumbling along in odd Wellingtons, while Dickie flapped over the damp grass in David's house slippers. Macbeth, of course, was ready for anything, and was extremely noisy.

"Hello," said David. "What woke *you* up? You were asleep, Dickie, when I came down . . ."

"So that's just it," panted Dickie. "Did you hear him, twin? Just what we thought . . ."

"Of course," said Mary. "Just what we thought.

Slinkin' out all quiet. Trickin' and trappin' us like he always does . . ."

"WHAT ARE YOU PLANNIN' OUT HERE WITH-OUT US?" demanded Dickie. "It's always like this, David, you beast."

"Seems to me," said Mary, "*us*, I mean. Seems to us that you don't think we're big enough to plan things. Well, WE ARE. Once and for all WE ARE, and we're jolly well going to . . ."

From the seat on the caravan steps, Fenella had been listening to the duet with astonishment. When there came at last a welcome pause, she put down her plate and went over to the twins, who were now scarlet in the face, and stood still looking at them. Under her steady gaze Dickie fidgeted and plucked at his twin's arm. But it was Reuben who saved the situation by picking up Macbeth's new basket and passing it to Mary.

"You have just come in time to see us off," he smiled. "Help us to pack and wish us luck when we go. See . . . ! Here is the travelling basket we promised for the little dog and here is a gift for your mother."

And for this, Mary gave him such a smile that he looked at her twice before going into the caravan to fetch some coloured cord.

"Tie the basket on the carrier with this," he said. "Now we must go. The sun will soon be hot and you must be away as well. Travel as lightly as you can. Do not trust the mountain, and wish us well . . . Come, Fenella *chi* . . ."

They all helped. Mary and Fenella rinsed the dirty plates in the stream while Reuben went to fetch the pony. Miranda cleaned up quickly and stamped on the still red embers of the fire.

Then the horse was harnessed at last and the three Romany climbed up to the driving seat. The twins ran ahead to open the gate as Reuben clicked his tongue and the van turned on the grass in front of Witchend. Mrs. Morton appeared on the porch.

Reuben removed his hat courteously and Miranda called

"Thank you, lovely lady," but Fenella stared straight ahead.

"Come along, David," Mrs. Morton said, "and fetch in those twins. I don't know what Agnes will say when she realizes they're not dressed properly . . . You're a silly chap, you know, for you've got lots to do yet . . ."

After breakfast the final preparations for the journey were hurried forward. The small, neat haversacks were carefully packed—pyjamas, spare shorts and shirts, washing things and toothbrushes, sandals instead of slippers, hand-kerchiefs (Dickie complained about the weight of these) and plenty of socks. David's pack was bigger and heavier, of course, and then the bicycle saddlebags were filled with camping odds and ends—all the things which they had learned from experience at Lone Pine were important—until all that was left was the bundle of sleeping bags and waterproofs which David had decided should be carried by Sally, Peter's pony.

But Sally proved troublesome. David caught her easily enough, for she knew him well by now, and they did not have much difficulty in saddling and bridling her. But when it came to fixing the bundles to her back, she ob-jected. She was a mountain-bred pony who knew Peter's mind and hands and hated anyone else on her back. David she tolerated, but to be a pack-horse had no appeal, and they had many struggles with her before she suffered the bundles to be strapped across the saddle.

At last the expedition was ready to start. With white, tense faces the twins stood by their bicycles as their mother came over and kissed them.

"Take care, David," she said. "And don't do anything stupid. Mrs. Sterling didn't say exactly how long you were to stay, but I can trust you not to overstay your welcome, and I expect you to come back with Peter and her father. . . . Good-bye, twins. Promise you'll be good and do what David says?"

"All right," said Dickie. "We swear."

"Thank you for letting us go," said Mary.

Then it was that David had his awful idea.

"What a fool I've been," he shouted. "What a fool! We oughtn't to take bikes, for we'll never get them across the Stiperstones. I'm sure we shan't. It's sure to be too steep and rough, and the twins couldn't possibly push loaded bikes up the mountain . . . And if we cycle round the longer way I don't think I can lead Sally all that distance. What shall we do?"

"Cycle as far as the road allows, David, and leave your cycles somewhere at the foot of the mountain to be called for. Didn't you say that there's an inn there? The twins must ride as far as they can."

And so it was decided. Macbeth, looking very woe-begone and apprehensive, was lifted into Reuben's basket now firmly fixed on Mary's carrier. It was a beautiful basket, but he hated it and jumped out three times. At last Mary spoke to him seriously and pointed out that unless he behaved himself he would have to be left behind. At this fearful threat, he put back his ears, showed the white of his eyes, and trembling all over, crouched down in his new carriage.

Then the cavalcade started.

"Lots of fun and come back soon," their mother called, and walked over to close the gate behind them.

David went first, cycling slowly, and leading the indignant Sally. It was a tricky and difficult task, and he wobbled ominously in the lane as he led the way down to Ingles with the twins chattering behind him. Then he realized that they had not yet heard from Tom, but, as they neared the farm gate, he saw Tom and his uncle cross the farmyard. He whistled the Peewit call and Tom stopped and looked up towards them. Then he ran over to the gate and Mr. Ingles himself followed slowly.

"'Mornin', young David, and to you two as well. Tom tells me you're off to visit Petronella over Stiperstones. We heard the old man had gone to Birmingham . . . HI! BETTY! COME OUT AND SEE MORTONS!" he roared suddenly.

The children all loved Mrs. Ingles, but David wanted

to get on and not stand gossiping, so after they had greeted her he said: "What about Tom, Mr. Ingles? Couldn't he come along with us now?"

Mrs. Ingles looked appealingly at her husband, who shook his head ruefully.

"Sorry," he said. "But can't be done now. No good young Tom playing at farming. He'll come over Saturday maybe—that is, if he's specially and properly asked for."

Then Mary sidled over to him.

"Mr. Ingles," she coaxed. "Dickie and me hate calling you that . . . Mr. Ingles, we mean. It sounds so grown-up and ugly. Only this morning Dickie and me were saying, 'Wish we could call Mr. Ingles Uncle Alf,' we said, didn't we, Dickie?"

"Yes, that's right, Mary. So we did. Just after we'd said our prayers. 'I do love Mr. Ingles,' you said. 'Wish we could call him Uncle Alf!' you said."

Mary nodded, gulped, and curled her little brown hand into the farmer's big, dirty one as she looked up at him with wide, dark-blue eyes. Mr. Ingles, who had no children of his own, cleared his throat, pushed his cap to the back of his head and reddened under his tan.

"That's easy enough, me dear," he muttered. "Uncle I am to young Tom here, and uncle I'll be to you two and proud of it, I'm sure."

There followed a moment's awkward silence as David turned away in embarrassment at this shameless exhibition, and Mrs. Ingles looked at the twins with a doubtful eye.

"Well, Uncle Alf," Mary went on in her clear little voice, "we shall like that very much, shan't we, Dickie?"

"Yes, Uncle Alf, we shall," came the echo.

"And so, Uncle, as this is rather a special sort of day, it would be rather nice if you'd 'low your other little nephew boy Tom to come with us today," and she looked up at him appealingly.

But Mr. Ingles, whose mind may have been a trifle slow on some matters, now seemed to sense the atmosphere and a glance at his wife's amused face confirmed this suspicion.

Suddenly he grinned and banged a huge fist to his knee.

"Dang my eyes!" he roared. "You young villains! 'Twas a try-on, I do believe, just to get young Tom some time off . . . Come here, young Mary, and I'll be an uncle to you . . ."

But by now the twins had retreated to a safe distance on the farther side of the gate. Mary was indignant.

"Oh, *no*, Uncle Alf. *Of course*, it wasn't because of Tom, although we'd like him to come now very much."

"Thanks, Mary," Tom muttered, "but I'm staying with Uncle. Maybe I'll come for the week-end."

"Well, we must get going," David said, glaring at the twins. "Good-bye, Mr. and Mrs. Ingles. 'Bye, Tom. You've got the address. Better send a wire to let us know when you're coming. 'Bye, all," and he pushed his bicycle to the grass verge, leading the protesting Sally behind him. "Come on, you two," he muttered fiercely. "You'd better go first. Straight up the hill and then turn right."

They breasted the hill and turned west along a well-made road. Progress was slow because of the difficulty of leading Sally, and they had to take frequent rests and at each halt Dickie demanded food.

After an hour's travelling they came to a village and the twins were left in charge of Sally while David went into the Post Office and sent Peter rather an expensive telegram, which read: "Expedition under way pack horse difficult meet at Devil's Chair today Lone Pine."

Not long after this halt they came to the lane of which Reuben had told them. Now they had their backs to the Long Mynd and the black rocks on the summit of Stiperstones in front of them took clearer shape. Sally was behaving better now, but David was very tired of leading her and the twins were usually about a quarter of a mile ahead. When at last he came to the "Hope Anchor" inn, it was to find Dickie and Mary already seated on a bench outside in the sun entertaining a rosy-faced woman who was wearing a print apron. In the hand of each twin was a half-full glass, and on the ground were two ginger-beer bottles.

As David came up it was to hear Dickie saying:

"*This* is our brother we were telling you about. If you ask him he will pay for the ginger-beer!"

The woman looked up and smiled.

"Well, I *was* surprised when I saw them come into the bar as bold as bold and say 'Two ginger pops, please, and our brother'll pay,' they said. And maybe you'd be enjoying a ginger-beer yourself, young sir?" she finished.

David said he would, and added, "And may we put the pony in your field just for a bit? We shan't be here long, but we'd like to eat our sandwiches out here in the sun if we may."

So the pack-horse was relieved of her burden and put out to grass while Dickie was, at long last, saved from starvation. When they had finished their sandwiches the sun had disappeared behind heavy thundery clouds and the air had become very still and heavy.

The woman came out again and chatted to them.

"Where'm you all going today?" she asked. "Weather going to be bad, I reckon. Thunder, I wouldn't be surprised. Better not go too far!"

When David told her that they were on their way to friends on the other side of the mountain and were meeting at the Devil's Chair, she looked surprised.

"But you're never going up over now? Ye are? It's a stiff climb and lonely, too, and the weather looks like breaking . . . And those cycles? Ye'll never get those over. Those little ones'll not be able to push them up, for the track is nothing but stones . . ."

David explained that they hoped they could leave the cycles with her and call for them on their way back in a few days' time. This was agreed without difficulty, but then they had to transfer the loaded saddlebags to Sally. This took a long time and David needed all his patience.

The pony was difficult and the twins were not helpful. Dickie kept chattering on about the Devil's Chair and what he was going to do when he got up there, and Mary was trying to make up her mind whether Macbeth could manage without his basket. The friendly hostess of the "Hope Anchor" helped, but by the time they were ready she looked anxiously up the mountain.

"Ye have to go? Ye can bide here if you wish and welcome. Weather looks bad."

"We've got to go," said Dickie. "You're afraid that old devil is comin' to his throne. Mary and me heard all about that. We were frightened 'bout him once last summer, but we're not now. When I get up there we're goin' to jump on his silly old chair."

Before the woman could reply to this boasting Mary chimed in.

"We've been wonderin', David, whether we ought to be tied up."

"Tied up? What d'you mean, Mary?"

"*You* know. Like they do when they climb mountains. They always do."

David assured them that this would not be necessary, and after several minutes' argument they tore themselves away from their new friend and started up the rough lane which she pointed out to them. After ten minutes the trees thinned out and they found themselves on the side of the mountain. The twins, who were in front, turned and looked down on the "Hope Anchor" lying below them like a little model from a toy shop.

"She's still there," said Mary. "Look, David. I think she's waving."

They waved in return, but David would not let them linger. He was not enjoying this journey very much, for he was tired already and not very used to Sally. Also it was horribly hot and the path, winding steeply now between the heather, was treacherous with loose stones. And the flies were a torment to the three travellers as well as to Sally, who was fidgety and unhappy. For a time it seemed as if the path was leading them away from the Chair and Mary complained that it was a magic mountain.

"Anyway," her twin said, "it's a beastly mountain, and I don't like it, and I wish we hadn't come. I hate it . . ."

Mary added, "David, we're going to stop. We're tired . . . An' it's no use you lookin' grumpy like that."

David crossly accepted this decision as they seemed to have come more than half-way and he needed a rest himself. Although they were so high, there was no breath of wind and the heat was stifling. Over behind the black rocks crowning the summit the sky was copper-coloured and the whole world seemed waiting for the storm which would not break. It may have been the weather, or it may, as David wondered to himself later, have been the influence of the mountain which had such a bad reputation, but from this moment they all started squabbling. Nothing went right as they continued the journey. The twins blamed him for bringing them this way, and even went as far as to say that they wished they had stayed at home. Then Dickie got a blister and Mary a stitch. But at last they toiled up to where the track turned to the right along the topmost ridge, above which were piled the black rocks of the summit.

"Gosh!" said Dickie. "It looks like another mountain on the top of this one. I s'pose you're going to force us to go up, David?"

"You can do what you jolly well like," snapped David. "I'm sick of both of you and your quarrelling. Of course, as soon as you see Peter, you'll both put on your best manners and be your silly, irritating selves and interrupt each other as usual . . . And why don't you let Mac walk, Mary, instead of carrying him round as if he'd lost the use of his legs? You spoil that dog. He can walk ten miles farther than you any day."

"You BEAST, David! You uttah beast! Look at him! He's dyin' of thirst almost in this vile place you've brought us to. Don't speak to us again. We hate you—all of us— me, and Dickie and Mackie, too!" and she burst into tears.

Mechanically, Dickie fumbled for a handkerchief, while David hated himself for being so snappy. Somehow he made his peace and they went on until even the heather was left behind and the track swung off to the left of the rocks towering above them.

"We'll rest here for a bit," David observed. "Peter would know the way we'd come, I expect, and I can't lug Sally up the rocks."

Mary seemed ready to rest again, but Dickie suddenly said:

"You two can stay here. I'm not afraid of the old devil. I'm going to climb up there and sit in his chair and watch for Peter."

"Dickie!" gasped Mary. "Aren't you afraid?"

"Awful," replied her twin. "I'm trembling all over, but I said I would, and I will. I jolly well will, and you'd better come too, twin . . . Then we can both be frightened, and it won't be so bad as me being frightened by myself."

Mary looked doubtful, then said, stoutly enough:

"All right, Richard, I'll come," and David knew this was a big decision, for it was only at such times that she called her twin by his full name.

Macbeth was now lying full stretch against a rock. His tongue was lolling and he was gasping for breath, and Sally was irritable and jumpy as she tried to rid herself of her burden and of the torment of flies. David knew that he dare not leave the pony and neither could he take her up the rocks.

"All right," he said. "If you can't find me give the Peewit call and I'll call you back. And for goodness sake be sensible and don't break your legs on the rocks. I think you're a couple of little idiots, but hurry up . . . Oh, and if you see Peter give me a call."

So the twins scrambled up out of sight, and David leaned back against the rocks in the little sheltered place he had found and slapped the flies off Sally.

It was hotter than ever and very still. The twins' voices died away somewhere over his head, and Macbeth panted at his feet. David half dozed for a minute or two and was roused by the Peewit call. At the same time Sally whinnied. David jumped awake and called in return, and a clear, cheerful voice cried:

"Where are you, David?"

It was Peter! And suddenly there she was on the track just below him, and he realized that she had come from the other side of the rocks.

"Hello, David. Here I am. Where are the others? Oh! and there's darling Sally . . . Have you been here long?"

They shook hands rather shyly and then, before David could answer, Macbeth whimpered and the storm broke with a shattering crash of thunder. They had no other warning but this. There were no preliminary mutterings and growlings in the distance and no tentative heavy splashes of rain to send them into shelter. The shock was so great that Peter put her hands over her ears and crowded back against David as the blue fire of the lightning crackled round them and Sally plunged and snorted in terror.

Then the rain came in solid sheets. Peter's shirt turned dark blue as David watched her stupidly and helplessly, and the water poured down his neck from the rocks against which he was leaning.

Another crash seemed to bring them to themselves, and Peter jumped forward to pet the pony.

"Where are the twins, David?" she shouted.

"They're up on the top there. Wait here with the animals, Peter. I must go and find them. Gosh! Look at the rain. They'll be wet through already and so am I. The little idiots! They would go."

Then, faint and far away in a lull between the thunder, came the Peewit's call for help and David darted out into the storm.

6. H.Q.2

WHEN MRS. STERLING came downstairs early next morning her kitchen seemed full of children. In the confusion of the Lone Piners' hectic arrival the previous evening, she had not had much opportunity of getting to know the Mortons. They had arrived wet, but noisy and cheerful, and owing to the shortage of beds at Seven Gates and to the fact that the barn was not yet ready for occupation, Mary and Macbeth had slept with Peter, and David and Dickie in the black horsehair sofa in the parlour. Mrs. Sterling, rather nervous about Uncle Micah's reactions, had hurried them upstairs and into hot baths. Then they had all enjoyed a picnic supper on Peter's bed and badgered her unsuccessfully to tell them about her mystery and the big surprise.

But Mrs. Sterling did not know all this. She had rather hoped to talk to Peter about the visitors before breakfast, but when she opened the kitchen door Peter was the only one not there. David was on his knees before the fire blowing the embers into flame, while the twins sat side by side on the table swinging their pyjamaed legs and advising him. Macbeth, on the hearthrug, was watching a large tabby cat with grave suspicion, but he cocked his ears and growled as she came into the room.

The twins turned and Mary said gravely:

"Good morning. How are you this morning, Mrs. Sterling?"

Before she could answer, Dickie added:

"Thank you. We are quite well, too, but we slept badly."

David sat back on his heels and smiled.

"I always do this at home if I'm the first down, so I hope

you don't mind. It'll be all right if we can just find some wood—I don't know where it is ... And don't take any notice of Dickie's rudeness, Mrs. Sterling. He always sleeps and eats well, but last night he wanted *all* the sofa, so I put him on the outside, and he fell off several times ... Now, if you'll tell us what else we can do to help, we'll get on with it."

"I don't think Seven Gates has ever had so many people to breakfast before. As you're here perhaps you'd better have yours first, before Mr. Sterling comes in from the farm. Where's Peter, by the way?"

"Asleep," said Mary. "Would you like us to go and wake her?"

"No," said David promptly. "Not both of you. Mary can go, and you get dressed, Dickie, but *don't* go together."

"Very well, David dear," said Mary sweetly.

And, "Excuse us," said Dickie, and they both went upstairs together, followed by Macbeth.

David looked at his hostess apologetically.

"I'm afraid there may be an awful row up there in a minute," he said. "They're going to be a nuisance today, I know ... It's awfully good of you to put us up like this, Mrs. Sterling. Peter kept hinting at a secret last night, but I hope we're not in the way."

Mrs. Sterling liked him for the way he spoke, and explained that they were welcome, but that they were short of beds. She hinted that other arrangements were being planned and that he would hear more later. Suddenly there came from upstairs two heavy bumps and a series of blood-curdling yells.

David pretended to look surprised, then: "I was afraid so, Mrs. Sterling. I believe they're Indians this morning. I should think Peter is a victim. If you'll excuse me I'll go and bang their heads together."

"Yes, do, David, and please hurry. I want breakfast over before Mr. Sterling comes in."

David dashed up the stairs and was just in time to see Dickie come hurtling backwards out of Peter's bedroom.

He was clasping a pillow, and as he slipped and fell, Mary followed and tried to help him up. Then Peter's door slammed and David heard the key turn.

"She's a cad!" gasped Dickie. "She winded me. Right in the tummy she threw it. We were only wakin' her up! That's all."

David grinned. "She was too much for you that time. Serves you both right. Now get dressed and don't make nuisances of yourselves." Then at Peter's door he called: "Buck up, Peter. Your aunt wants you, and we're to have breakfast before Mr. Sterling appears. We're all starving and have been up for hours."

"Have those little beasts gone? They poured water out of the tooth-glass down my neck while I was asleep . . . All right, David, I shan't be a tick. I expect you'll find Henry and Humphrey out in the yard. You'll like them."

So David went outside and said "Hello" to the farm-hands who seemed deeply shocked at the sight of another visitor. But surprise turned to alarm when the twins and Macbeth bounced out a few minutes later.

"Look at 'em, Henery. Look at 'em and tell me if you see what I see," Humphrey whispered.

"As like as two peas . . ." replied his awestruck mate.

"In a pod and all . . ." finished Dickie brightly.

"My name is Mary Morton, and this is my brother Dickie," began Mary in the usual strain, and David, who had witnessed the performance many times, turned away in disgust. He gave Henry and Humphrey about five minutes before they surrendered.

Back in the kitchen Peter was now helping her aunt. Bacon was sizzling in the pan and the fire was blazing merrily.

"Did you find them, David? They're fun, aren't they? Cut some bread, will you?"

A call of "Breakfast ready" brought Dickie in at a run. Mary followed more slowly, and although Peter had laid a place for David between the twins, she sidled quickly in next to Dickie and said dreamily:

"You saw the nice fat one, David? Well, I've asked him to come and stay with us at Witchend."

Dickie's knife clattered onto his plate, but he quickly recovered himself.

"That's right," he said. "He's nice. We love him very much."

"But you can't do *that*," Mrs. Sterling said. "Of course he can't come and stay with you. Why—Mr. Sterling wouldn't let him . . ."

Before David could tell Mrs. Sterling not to take any notice of this sort of conversation, Mary started again:

"Where *is* Mr. Sterling? I want to see your uncle, Peter! Dickie and me have been talkin' about him and wondering whether he wants cheering up."

"P'raps we could go and find him when I've finished my breakfast?" from Dickie.

"No, no," Aunt Carol said, "you mustn't do that. You'll see him some time, I expect, but he's busy now. He'll be in presently. Finish up your breakfast like a good little boy and then Peter has got a surprise for you all."

The twins glanced at each other meaningly. They were never impressed by vague promises of surprises, but without further ado they launched into a descriptive duet of their adventures on the Devil's Chair. Peter and David were unable to check them, and as this was really the first time that Mrs. Sterling had experienced the twins in action, she was too fascinated to interrupt.

"I think you ought to know 'bout our adventure," Dickie began. "Well—comin' up the mountain, Mary and me swore a deadly oath that we'd dance in that old Devil's Chair, and we would have done that only his curse must have come upon us . . . Just as we came to the last and worst bit, the old Devil said, 'No, you don't, Dickie and Mary . . .' "

" 'Just get out o' my throne,' he said."

"And then, before we could do anything else, and I could leap up there and dance like we said we would in our oath, there was an awful crash and blue lightning . . ."

"Goin' bang, crackle, BANG all round us . . ."

"Gosh! it was awful, but we were brave, and then the rain came and more lightnings came *out* of the throne . . . Well, it was pretty awful, and so we made a secret call we know and thought we ought to be getting along . . ."

"'Cos we were afraid you would be kept waiting, Mrs. Sterling."

"An' then it lightninged and thundered again like in the Bible, and we started to come back, and brave David came and rescued us, and down we came . . ."

"And there was Peter just like a miracle."

As Mary finished triumphantly and wiped her mouth there came an awful noise from the doorway behind them.

"What is this prattle of miracles? And what is the meaning of this breaking of our peace?"

David got up and said, "Good morning, sir."

Peter blushed and said: "These are my friends, Uncle. I told you they were coming, but we shan't disturb you, I promise."

Aunt Carol rose. "Come and sit down, Micah, and I'll bring your breakfast. The children can go outside now. . . . Show them your surprise, Peter, and I'll come and help you presently."

Mary said suddenly: "I'm not going. I want to talk to Uncle Micah. I like him, and I think he wants cheering up," and she gave him the dazzling smile that was usually more than enough for most strangers.

"All right, Mary," said Dickie, "we'll stay. You two big ones can go and play somewhere, but mind you don't plan things."

And although Uncle Micah took no notice of these arrangements for his entertainment, Peter nodded briefly to David and the two rose from the table.

Outside in the sunshine Peter took a deep breath.

"Gosh, David! He's pretty awful, isn't he? Let's leave

him to the twins, 'cos I've lots to tell you, and before they
come out I'll tell you my secret . . . It isn't that I don't
want them here, but you know what they are, and it will
do them good to see it after we've been over it together.
. . . Come on!" and she led him over to the white-doored
barn.

"Well," said David, "what's the idea? They're fine big
doors, but what's inside?"

"Listen, David. I couldn't tell you properly last night
because everything was a muddle, and we were all wet
through and Aunt Carol thought that although we were
short of beds we ought to be indoors . . . You don't know
how thrilled I am that you're here, David. I would have
been jolly lonely without you all, because although Aunt
Carol is nice, I can't really find out why I've been asked
here except that Uncle is a bit odd and has always wanted
to see me 'cos I'm his only niece. And he is a bit peculiar,
David, because he seems to wander about a lot, and although he's been quite decent he stares at me, and sometimes I don't know what to say to him. Sometimes I think
he's frightened of something, and I'm sure he's unhappy.
And he makes Aunt Carol unhappy, too, but she was
pleased for you all to come . . . David, I do hope Dickie
and Mary won't make him mad. If they upset him he
might send you all back, and if he did that I think I'd
run away with you. And that reminds me of something
else . . ."

"Here, Peter, hold on! I don't know where I am, you
talk so fast. I thought you were going to show me something
about the barn. What's the matter with it?"

Peter fumbled in her shorts and produced a rolled-
up handkerchief. Inside the handkerchief was a key.
She unlocked the padlock and swung back the big white
doors.

"There you are," she said triumphantly. "Here's my
surprise for the Lone Piners! It's an indoor camp for us all,
and we can live and cook and eat and sleep here. It was my
idea, and except for some cleaning and clearing up which

we shall have to do this morning, it's practically ready. What do you think of it, David?"

David, never demonstrative, actually squeezed her arm.

"Peter! It looks super! It's marvellous. And we can sleep here, too? That's grand, because I'm not too keen on another night with Dickie on the sofa. I wouldn't mind sleeping here alone if it comes to it."

"Well, you're not going to sleep here alone. Don't be so mean. There's room for us all and there's an upstairs, too. Come and look."

When the doors were opened their widest, David could see the great oak pillars springing from the brick floor and passing through the flat ceiling. On the left of the centre "aisle" were the old grain stores with their partitions dividing them.

"These are the bedrooms, David. You can see that, can't you? I think it's dry, and presently we'll get some hay and pile it on the floor. Then if you use your sleeping-bags you'll be warmer than you were at home. On the other side, David, I thought we'd have our dining-room, and so I've asked Aunt Carol if we can borrow a table and she said yes. Then . . . but look here, David . . . this is the best of all. Look at this stove. We can have a fire here at nights and cook everying we want. Here's an old saucepan and a frying-pan that Aunt Carol lent me, and if we get a big enough fire we can take off this lid thing at the top and cook that way. I collected some wood yesterday. Shall we try it?"

"It's marvellous, Peter, but I think we'd better wait till the kids are here."

"Of course. That was rather mean of me. Now come upstairs, because I think that's the best of all. By the way, David, I've bagged to sleep up there."

When he had climbed the stairs and looked at the wide floor space, he said:

"Gosh, Peter, what *couldn't* we do up here? What's that pile of hay up by the window?"

"I put it there. I'm going to sleep up here, David, and

Mary can come with me if she likes, but I've bagged by the window. Come and look out. You can see right down into the village."

David knelt down on the litter and peered through the dusty pane. Peter was right. Not only could he see the side door of the house and practically everything in the farmyard, but he could look over the treetops to the roofs of Barton Beach a mile away where the morning sun glinted on the weathercock on the church steeple as the wind changed direction. Then, as he glanced down the door of the house opened.

"Peter," he whispered, forgetting that they could not be overheard. "Here! Look!"

Peter flopped down beside him and pushed him over so that she could see better. Then she gasped as Uncle Micah appeared with a twin holding each hand. Although they could not hear what was being said, it seemed that an animated conversation was in progress. Any conversation in which the twins took part was likely to be lively, as she knew, but she was surprised to see Uncle Micah pat Dickie on the head and then grimace behind his beard.

"Look at him, David! When he does that, he's smiling. He is, really! I saw him do it once before . . . But, David —they mustn't come here. We left the barn doors open, and I don't want him to see what we've done. He may have forgotten that he told Aunt Carol we could use the barn. Let's close the doors before they come round this way."

They rushed down.

"You take one door, Peter, and I'll do the other. Quick!"

Mary's clear treble sounded very near as they swung the doors together and stood with their ears to the crack.

"Now we've really met you we think we'd better call you Uncle Micah . . ."

"Oh, yes," said Dickie. "Everyone calls us by our proper names, like Dickie and Mary, and not Morton, like at school. So it'll be easier if we say Uncle . . ."

"'Specially as we'll see each other such a lot while

we're here," Mary continued brightly. "Jus' you let us know when you're feeling lonely, and we'll come along and be with you and bring Mackie, too . . ."

"We don't mind a *bit* . . . It's really a pleasure. We often cheer up people. We cheer up Uncle Jasper Sterling —Peter's daddy, you know—quite a lot . . ."

Uncle Micah's bass rumble died away and Peter gestured upstairs. From the look-out window they saw the oddly-assorted group turn through the white gate leading to the potato field. Macbeth, a disconsolate little black shadow, followed this unexciting procession without enthusiasm.

David whistled. "I believe they've done it again, Peter. They're uncanny. They can charm anybody—but I'd like to know why they're taking so much trouble over him."

"So would I, David. But if they can do anything to stop Uncle looking so gloomy and make him like an ordinary, decent sort of uncle who would be glad to have people like us here having fun in his barns—well, then, it'll be a good thing if they stay out with him all the morning. Oh, look! here's Aunt Carol. Let's go down."

Mrs. Sterling was leaning on the gate watching one large and two small figures disappear down the cart-track. As David and Peter crossed the yard, she turned and laughed.

"Oh, Peter," she called, "you did recommend the twins, didn't you? They're wonderful! They make him *laugh*, and I haven't seen him do that for months."

"What did they do?" asked David.

"Well, David, I don't know that they did anything particular except chatter all the time—mostly together. They told us about your journey yesterday and said you got very over-tired and snappy, but that they helped you along and cheered you up. When they said they would go round the farm with him, I thought he'd be angry, but he wasn't, and said they were welcome . . . I like your twins, David. They're grand . . . Now let's finish off the barn."

And David, who usually pretended to be a little ashamed of the twins and their antics, reddened at this praise of them and promised himself that he would remember to tell their mother.

Then they went back to the barn and he soon found that Mrs. Sterling was a very practical person and quick to understand what they wanted. While Peter undid the sleeping-bags and bundles and spread them on the clean hay, he got out his note-book and made a list of the things they would still need.

> "Three hurricane lamps (one for the girls upstairs).
> Coke and coal for stove (Lone Piners to pay for this).
> Water containers (a barrel would be grand).
> Matches (sorry, we forgot to bring any).
> Books (if the weather is bad. Sorry, we didn't bring ours).
> Sack of potatoes.
> Three more chairs (if possible).
> Cupboard for stores.

"I expect we shall think of lots of other things," David said. "We're awfully sorry to be such a nuisance . . . and . . . and if you don't mind me saying so, Mrs. Sterling, we do think it's jolly decent of you to help and lend us all these things. Don't we, Peter?"

"Yes, David, we do. If it hadn't been for Aunt Carol we'd never have got this place. Uncle first of all said this barn was never to be opened, but somehow Auntie won him over."

"Oh, well," her aunt smiled, "if I hadn't, the twins would have done. Now let me see the list . . . Hm! The lamps can be borrowed from the other barn. You'll find them on the wall, and the paraffin tank is in the yard at the back of the house. See that the wicks are trimmed, and don't overfill the lamps. You can have what coke and coal you want—that's at the back of the house, too. I shouldn't think we've got a barrel, so you had better borrow a big pail from the dairy. Water from the well. Matches are possible, but you must be careful with them, and you'd better be responsible, David. Books? Good idea. Borrow as many of mine as you like. I've got lots."

Mrs. Sterling went down the list. "Potatoes? Easy. Henry or Humphrey will let you have a sack. An old cupboard we can manage, I fancy, but I've no more chairs, though I think there's a hammock in the attic. Come on, David. Bring your list and a pencil and we'll go and see what we can find."

And so the wonderful indoor camp was got together. They fetched sticks and fir cones from the wood, and lit the fire, and then dashed out to see how the chimney was drawing. It wasn't, and the barn soon filled with choking smoke. David borrowed a ladder from the rickyard, and found an old nest built snugly into the top of the iron pipe, and when he had pulled this out the fire burned well. Peter found Grumpy pottering about and got him to bring over a sack of potatoes. The hammock was a great success, and they slung that low from two of the oak pillars facing the stove. Then when they had got in everything, Mrs. Sterling found them some eggs and told them to get on now and cook their own lunches.

"And didn't you say something about another friend, Peter? Tom, was it? Tom Ingles? Why don't you ask him for the week-end? He'll be no trouble while you're all here. I'll write a note to his mother. Oh, aunt, isn't it? . . . Well I'll write now and you can post it in the village this afternoon . . . Good-bye. I don't want to see any more of you for a long time."

When she had left them, David turned to Peter.

"I thought you didn't like this place? I agree that Uncle is a rum old bird, but I do like your aunt. I was thinking, Peter. We'll call this Headquarters Number Two, and it's thanks to you we've got it . . . Listen. Here come the twins. I wonder what they've done with Uncle?"

Dickie and Mary came through the gate, stopped as one man when they saw the others, and then advanced more slowly. But upon this occasion Dickie had more to say than his twin. Mary made one or two attempts to take her usual share in the abuse hurled at their elders for keeping a secret from them, but she seemed to be thinking of something else most of the time.

When David was able to make himself heard, he said, "No need to make such a noise, Dickie. What you both ought to be doing is thanking Peter who planned this place and has got it ready for us all with Mrs. Sterling. It's a fine indoor camp for the Lone Piners, and we're going to call it Headquarters Number Two. We're going to eat here and sleep here, too. Now just be quiet and look round and see how lucky we are. There's an upstairs, too, where the girls will sleep . . ."

This was quite a long speech for David, and it silenced the twins, although Dickie grimaced horribly to Mary to signify his disgust.

But there was plenty still to do and for the next two hours David kept them busy. Everything was unpacked and Peter, cook to the Lone Piners, got all the kitchen utensils together. Fresh water was fetched from the well and two big dairy pails filled. Then there was fuel to be got in and Dickie was put in charge of this department, and after some muttering and grumbling to the effect that "everyone was unfair to him", he slipped off to the house. When he returned he was carrying a large sheet of white paper and a hammer. By sign he indicated that his mouth was full of nails, and then, with a great deal of fuss, he fixed the paper to the white door of the barn. It showed the pine cone symbol and underneath was printed PRIVATE, H.Q.2.

After this had been duly admired, Peter produced the frying-pan, and soon Dickie's moodiness vanished as H.Q.2 was filled with the delicious savour of fried potatoes and onions. Mary offered to help, but when Peter said, "Not for a bit, thanks, I've got to learn this stove first," the little girl called Macbeth and wandered upstairs. When the eggs had been fried last of all and Peter had broken one plate and burned her fingers on the others, she asked Dickie to bang the kettle as a gong.

Meanwhile, David had put up the trestle table, and as the sun came streaming through the open doors the barn looked jollier and more inviting than it had for many years.

When they had all dealt with the first course, David looked up and said, "We must write to Tom and ask him to come this week-end. Then let's go down to Barton Beach together. We haven't seen it yet."

"All right," said Peter. "That's a good idea, but do you all think we might enlist another member? It's just as you say, but there's a girl called Jenny in the village. She's fun and has helped me a lot already, and I know she'd love to join. Of course, she's rather silly about the mountain, and she won't go near the Devil's Chair even in the daytime, but she does know all about the country, and knows lots of stories, too. And she keeps on running away from home . . ."

David looked up in surprise. "What's that got to do with it?"

"Nothing really, except that she's unhappy at home and likes adventures . . . I say, let's write her a secret note saying that if she would like to be a member she must be at the first white gate tonight at five o'clock."

They all agreed with enthusiasm, but for once Mary remained silent.

"What's wrong, Mary? You've hardly said a word for hours. Got a tummy ache?" asked Peter.

Mary looked scornful and made no reply, but later, when she was helping Peter wash up, the latter tried again to see what was worrying the little girl.

"It's Uncle Micah, Peter. I didn't say it in front of the others, 'cos they think I'm silly—even Dickie thinks I'm a bit silly . . . But he's so sad and lonely, Peter. It's awful how lonely he is. I don't think he's a wicked old man. I think he's just miserable and lonely, and I keep on remembering him when I ought to be doin' something else and having fun. We tried to cheer him up, Peter, and he nearly laughed once or twice, and then he told us—and he sort of told us as if we weren't there at all—about his big grown-up son that he's lost . . ." She dropped her voice to an awestruck whisper . . . "Charles has broken his heart, Peter. It's awful, and I wish I could help him."

Peter did not laugh. She was very fond of Mary and knew how sensitive she was. It was odd, but she also had had this feeling of pity for the old man, and so she tried to change the subject and was helped when David and Dickie came in with the letters they had been writing. The first was to Tom, telling him to be sure to come at the week-end and warning him that the way over the mountain would be difficult.

The other letter was a fearful and ill-spelled invitation to the prospective new member from Dickie. It was a frightening document, but Peter assured them that Jenny enjoyed exciting reading, so they decided to deliver it. Mary then ran in to Mrs. Sterling and got the letter for Mrs. Ingles, confirming Tom's invitation, and the four, with an excited Macbeth, set off for Barton Beach.

On the way down through the woods Mary recovered her usual spirits, and by the time the party had reached the village their plans had been made for delivering the summons to Jenny. Peter and David went into the baker's to buy some buns, while the twins, thoroughly primed, went into the post office to do battle with Mrs. Harman.

The bell clanged and their entrance was marred when Mary tripped over the top step.

They stood alone in the dark shop. As the echoes of the bell died away a phantom voice said harshly: "Well, what do you want?"

Mary squeezed Dickie's hand, gulped and then said loudly and clearly: "Whoever you are and wherever you are—I WANT A STAMP."

The curtains at the back of the shop opened and Mrs. Harman glowered at her small customers. Instantly Dickie turned his back and went over to the counter near the window, and as the woman groped for a stamp, Dickie declaimed in a loud voice, "I want a ball of string." He continued to demand a ball of string and when Mrs. Harman shouted to him to be quiet, Mary asked her for another stamp, while Dickie continued to utter his plaint that all he asked for was a ball of string. The pandemonium brought the desired result, for the curtains parted again to show Jenny's startled face under its tousled mop of red hair.

"Where have you been hiding, miss?" Mrs. Harman screamed. "Come and take a turn here and help me."

So Jenny ran across to Dickie, who immediately leaned over the counter and croaked in an unrecognizable voice out of the side of his mouth.

"Your name Jenny? Don't answer. Just nod."

Jenny nodded violently, and Dickie suddenly shouted: "NO. IT'S THICK STRING I GOTTA HAVE!" Then from the side of his mouth again, "I gotta secret message. Here it is. Hide it. Read it in secret and come tonight."

Then Mary's voice came loud and sweet from the post office counter:

"Thank you *so* much for all you've done. It's only one stamp I want after all. Are you ready, Dickie? Isn't this a funny shop?"

And Dickie said, "Thank you VERY much. It's not that sort of string I want. I need red string."

They turned together and smiled sweetly as Dickie opened the door so that the jangling of the bell drowned Mrs. Harman's angry voice. Then they went out hand in hand into the sunshine, smug in the satisfaction of work well done.

The farmyard was empty when they got back and there were no signs of Uncle Micah or Henry or Humphrey. They were only just able to make up the fire and lay the table before it was time to go back through the woods to meet Jenny.

But she came. As they watched her coming up the lane, Peter whispered to David, "She's plucky, David. She's frightened and she hates it—you can see she is—but she's made up her mind to go through with it."

Jenny was whistling and pretending she did not care, but her whistle was very quavery. After a long pause she found the courage to open the gate and step into the wood. In a flash the twins broke from cover and dived for her legs. Down came Jenny, and almost before she could struggle a bandage was over her eyes.

"Not a word," growled Dickie.

As they led her through the wood, Peter said:

"It's all right, Jenny. Just be sensible and you'll come to no harm."

"You're taking me up to Seven Gates," Jenny replied. "I don't want to go there, and why can't I have this thing off my eyes?"

"No," said David, "you can't till we tell you. You're going to be asked to do something, and if you refuse you'll be taken back again blindfolded."

"Oh, well," Jenny remarked reasonably enough, "I can only die once, I s'pose, but don't take me too far, 'cos I've got a bad stitch and I've got to be home soon. I've run away again just to be in this adventure, so do buck up and get it over."

But they didn't take the bandage off till Jenny was seated in the hammock in the barn, and then she looked round with astonishment.

"These are your friends, aren't they, Peter?" she said after a long stare at the twins.

Then they told her all about the Lone Pine Club and asked if she would like to join.

"You'd really let me be a real member? But that's wonderful, and I'd love it, and thank you very much, and I'll do anything you say. Except go up the Dingle at night," she added.

So David told her the rules and she signed on a page of his note-book. Dickie insisted that she sign in her own blood as the original members had done, and Mary went to the house to borrow a needle. Then they told her about the Peewit whistle and how it was their secret call and promised to let her know about the next meeting at the week-end to meet Tom.

And when she had to go they went down with her to the first gate. She ran off and turned at the corner to call a plaintive "Peewit . . . Peeewit."

"I like her, Peter," David said as they walked home up the hill. "She's a sport. I wonder how she'll get on with Tom?"

Mrs. Sterling was waiting in the yard for them, but only to see if they were all right. Mary asked after Uncle Micah, and was told that he'd got one of his bad heads and had gone upstairs and that was all she would say.

So they said good night to her and thanked her for all she had done, and Peter ran after her because she looked so lonely and gave her a special hug and asked her to come and have some cocoa with them round the stove. She thanked them, but said, "Another night, perhaps," and then told them not to get up too early.

It was while they were having their cocoa that Mary fell asleep in the hammock. David looked up suddenly to see her slumping sideways and grabbed the mug as the grip of her fingers relaxed. They were all tired after an exciting day so they agreed to go early to bed.

The stove was made safe and Mary and Peter went upstairs. Mary slipped quickly into her pyjamas and snuggled into her fleecy sleeping-bag. She saw Peter kneeling by the window, and was reminded to say an apologetic little prayer herself, and then she put out her hand to feel Macbeth at her side and fell instantly asleep.

It was some hours later that she woke with the feeling that something was going to happen. She had these feelings sometimes about Dickie and with Dickie, but it was not that now. The moon shone full on her face. The yard below was picked out in black and silver, and Peter was breathing peacefully a yard away. Then Macbeth stirred, and Mary, with a hand on his neck, felt the suspicion of a growl start in his throat. She was wide awake now and knelt up in the sleeping-bag to look out of the window. And, as she watched, the door of the house opened and Uncle Micah stood, a lonely figure, in the moonlight. He turned his head to look up at the mountain, and with a shock Mary saw his face. It was blank, expressionless, frightening.

She shivered. "He looks as if he's asleep," she thought. "He's lonely."

The old man closed the door silently, and with quick, mechanical steps crossed the yard and passed out of sight. Just for a second she wondered whether to wake Peter, and then she thought, "No. This is Dickie and me. This is another adventure for us," and without another thought she scrambled into her clothes. At the top of the stairs she stopped and ran back for her heavy sweater, then she crept down into the barn.

The moonlight was slanting in through the windows here and a cinder fell in the stove as she passed. She could hear David breathing gently in the far corner. She was just wondering how best to wake Dickie when a shadow over by the door moved. Mary's heart was thudding so hard that her body seemed to shake, and she held her breath in suspense. Then she realized that Macbeth was at her side and that his tail was wagging against her leg. The shadow moved again, and Dickie padded across the floor into a patch of moonlight, struggling into his sweater as he came.

"What is it, twin?" he whispered. "Adventure for us?"

Mary nodded, and without another word they crept to the great doors and slipped out into the night. Hand in hand, two tiny figures dwarfed by the great buildings, and the mountains above them, they stood listening in the moonlight. Then, clear but far away, came a sharp click.

"That's the latch of that little white gate, Mary . . . the one leading to the Dingle . . . you know . . ." and together they turned in that direction.

A little black dog trotted at their heels.

7. The Black Messenger

DAVID SLEPT DREAMLESSLY. He had always enjoyed camping and preferred the feel of a sleeping-bag and the smell of the hay to the springs of a bed and the freshness of sheets. He did not even turn over until the sun was up and Henry and Humphrey were starting work in the yard. Dimly he heard the drone of their slow voices as the horses clumped out of the stable, and when one of the men began to whistle he looked at his watch. Just past seven and time somebody was moving. He wondered whether the girls were up, but could not hear any sound from upstairs. Then he remembered that Dickie had been told to get the stove ready for Peter and that he ought to be getting to work by now.

David listened for his brother's breathing, but there was no sound from the other side of the partition.

"Dickie," he called, "time to get up."

There was no answer, so David reached out for a shoe and tossed it over. As this produced no result, he wriggled out of his bag and called again sharply: "Dickie, get up and stop playing the goat."

But before he could get an answer Peter's voice came from the top of the stairs:

"What's the matter, David? Isn't Dickie there? Mary's gone, too."

He looked up, saw Peter's rather anxious face above him, and ran round into Dickie's division. It was empty and his sleeping-bag lay limply on the hay.

"Have they taken Mackie?" Peter asked, as she ran down the steps and across the floor to the great doors which David was pushing back. Together they whistled for the dog, but there was no response.

"Well, I'm going to get some clothes on." Peter announced. "Wait for me and we'll get the fire going. They'll be back for breakfast, I'm sure."

David went outside to wash in a pail. He was combing the water out of his hair when Peter came out into the sunshine again.

"What's for breakfast?" he said. "I'm hungry. And what shall we do today? I suppose Tom will get his letter this afternoon. I'll be glad when he comes and we're all together again."

"Oh, yes," Peter said. "I like Tom. What d'you think of Jenny, David?"

"I don't think she'd be much use in what Dickie would call a 'crissis,' but she's good fun. We'll try and meet her today somehow. I do wish these kids wouldn't play the fool, but we jolly well won't wait breakfast for them . . . Come on . . . I'll do the fire and you can get busy."

He soon got the fire alight and Peter got to work with the frying-pan, and then David searched the farmyard again and even went down into the wood to whistle Macbeth. By the time he got back he was furious. As he entered the barn Peter called:

"I've cooked theirs, too, but it's difficult without an oven. There's no way of keeping it hot."

"If they're not here by the time I've finished mine I'll eat theirs too," David growled, and then went outside again and beat upon an empty saucepan. And this time he did get an answer, for round the corner of the house came Uncle Micah looking haggard in the morning sunlight. David dropped the wooden spoon with which he had been beating the gong and stared in amazement at the old man's unkempt appearance. His black eyes were wild and restless and fixed themselves on David almost unseeingly, while his hands plucked at his beard.

"What means this clamour?" he boomed suddenly, and David felt rather than heard Peter come out of the barn and stand beside him.

"Good morning, Uncle Micah," she began. "That's our

gong. We're just going to have breakfast. Would you like to see how we've tidied up the barn and made it ship-shape for our camp?"

The old man passed his hand across his eyes and then said:

"Those two . . . I want to see those two . . . the two little ones."

"You mean Dickie and Mary? Oh! They're off together somewhere. Why do you want to see them, Uncle?"

"Tell them to come to me. I shall be in the twenty-acre over the mountain . . . As soon as they come back tell them, I pray . . ." and he strode away towards the house.

Peter looked worried as they went back into the barn and took two plates from the top of the stove. They sat down at the table in silence, and although the sun was shining right into the barn through the wide-open doors their meal was a gloomy one.

Every now and then, between mouthfuls, David would mutter, "Silly young idiots."

At last Peter put down her knife and fork and said:

"For goodness' sake, cheer up, David. I can't think what's the matter with you . . . they're only having a bit of fun . . ." but she said this as if she didn't really mean it, and when David glanced up with a "Sorry, Peter," he caught a very worried look on her face. Before he could say any more, there came a cheerful greeting from behind them.

"Good morning, all. My word, but you must have a fine cook here—your breakfast smells good . . ."

David got up, and Peter smiled.

"Come and have a cup of tea with us, Aunt Carol."

"Thank you, I will. Your uncle was late for his breakfast and I'd had mine. Where are the twins, by the way? He said he wanted to see them, but I can't imagine why."

"Oh, they're just playing one of their silly tricks, Mrs. Sterling. They often do this sort of thing, but I must admit that Dickie has never been known to miss a meal if he can help it."

"What do you mean, David?" she asked, as Peter passed

her a cup and she sat down gingerly in the hammock.
"What sort of tricks?"

"I'm going to say what I think, David." said Peter.
"I'm sorry I didn't say it before, but I believe they must
have gone out in the middle of the night and not just before
we got up at seven this morning."

"But Peter—how do you know?" her aunt said.

"Oh, I don't *know*, Auntie. I'm sorry I'm so silly and
I can't really believe that anything is *wrong*, but . . . but
when I went up to dress I felt Mary's sleeping-bag and it
was quite cold and when David was washing outside, I felt
Dickie's too and that was cold . . ."

"You didn't say anything, Peter. Why didn't you . . . ?"

Peter's voice rose. "Oh, I don't know *why*. It was silly,
I know, and wrong too, but I s'pose I wanted to believe
that they'd just gone out and that they'd be back in a
tick . . ."

"Yes, Peter," said her aunt quietly, "what else? You've
got something else on your mind, haven't you?"

Peter stood up with a queer look in her eyes.

"Yes, I have. Ever since I got up I've been trying to
remember a dream . . . I suppose it was a dream but the
moon was shining over me and Mary too . . . I'm sure it
was Mary 'cos her curls shone all silvery in the moonlight.
She bent over me and smiled a worried little smile, and
I sort of felt that she was trying to tell me something, but
though I struggled to wake up and speak to her I just
couldn't move and . . ."

David, who was listening enthralled as he watched her
puzzled face, suddenly saw her blue eyes widen and fix
themselves on something behind him. Her hand went to
her mouth in a gesture of bewilderment and fear, and as
she stopped speaking David wheeled and saw Uncle Micah
standing on the threshold. He stood like some grotesque
statue with an odd, listening expression on his face. His
lips twitched and then, as he realized that they had all
seen him, he turned and strode away into the sunshine
with a sort of pathetic guiltiness.

Mrs. Sterling jumped to her feet and followed him, but called over her shoulder:

"I'll come back. Don't do anything silly."

When she had gone, Peter sat down suddenly and, rather like the twins, started fumbling for a handkerchief. David saw that she was trembling and that there was a suspicion of tears in her eyes.

"I'm sorry, David. Silly of me . . . But, David, we must *do* something quickly I'm sure. Something has happened to the twins, I believe, and it's up to us to go and find them. . . . *David, I believe Uncle Micah knows where they are or something about them* . . . He looked as if he knew . . ."

David nodded. "Yes. He did look funny."

"Listen, David! We'll leave everything here and pack up the knapsack with food 'cos I bet Dickie's hungry, and go and search for them. They can't be very far away and anything is better than waiting about here for them to turn up."

Peter was so much in earnest and so anxious that David soon agreed and together they packed up some food in one of the knapsacks. Then they went over to the house, and there was Aunt Carol making some cakes and behaving as if nothing unusual had happened this morning. She made no reference to Uncle Micah, but when Peter told her what they intended to do, she said:

"Yes, I think that's sensible enough. You know these twins better than I do, but I think they've been exploring somewhere on their own and now they've got tired and have gone to sleep in the sun. I should make one or two discreet inquiries in the village first and it wouldn't be a bad idea to take Jenny along with you so that you can use her as a messenger either to here or to Barton Beach . . . But don't worry yourselves. The twins can't come to any harm and they'll soon turn up. Good luck!"

David ran back to the barn for his knife and his notebook before they went off together through the wood and down to the village. There were not many people about in Barton Beach, but the silent man from the garage was leaning against his petrol pump.

"Good morning," said Peter brightly. "Have you seen a small boy and girl—twins—about nine—with a little black dog round here this morning?"

"No," the man said without turning his head.

"He couldn't very well say less," David remarked as they strolled on towards the Post Office. "How are we going to get hold of Jenny, by the way? Would you like me to try and manage it. The old dame doesn't like you, does she?"

But before Peter could answer, a bell clanged, the door of the Post Office opened, and Jenny herself appeared. She was wearing blue jeans and carrying a heavy pail of water which she set down with a crash on the pavement.

David whistled the Peewit call until Jenny looked up in surprise and crossed the road to them.

"Hello!" she said. "You *are* early. She says I'm to clean the windows and I was just thinking I wouldn't."

"I wouldn't either," said Peter.

"I shouldn't think they're dirty anyway," said David. "Nobody would notice it."

"Why have you come?" asked Jenny. "And where are those two funnies?"

"You haven't seen them about, have you, Jenny?" Peter went on. "They've run off somewhere for a lark and we're looking for them. We wondered if you'd come and help us search . . . Of course we couldn't possibly ask you to run away from home again, but this is a job for the Lone Piners and you ought to be in it."

David continued, "We've no idea where they've gone, but Macbeth is obviously with them so we think they're off on one of their adventures. They do the craziest things together sometimes, but as Dickie hasn't come back for his breakfast it looks as if they've lost themselves. We don't want to make a fuss up at Seven Gates yet but we must start looking for them . . . Will you come with us, Jenny? Peter says you know the country round here and we can do with a guide."

Jenny nodded violently. "I should think I can. I'll just run away as usual. Come on! Where shall we go?"

Peter said:

"I've been thinking. We don't really know where to go first, but I believe that if those two have gone off on their own, they would go up Black Dingle. We came down that way and it leads to the Devil's Chair that Dickie wants to dance on . . ." here there was a gasp from Jenny . . . "and it's also the most likely place to explore. I think we ought to search the Dingle first and look for a clue. If we're not lucky this afternoon we must tell the grown-ups. What do you think?"

David nodded agreement. "Sounds sensible to me. Let's go, but I'll hurry on and slip up through the wood just to see if they've come home . . . You can wait for me by that old signpost. Can you come now, Jenny, or shall we wait at the top of the street for you?"

"No. I'll come now, but we'd better hurry else she'll find out that I'm not doing those old windows."

David ran on ahead, and the two girls watched him disappear up the hill. Jenny chattered all the way, but Peter was too worried to say much. She was very uneasy and, after they had passed the first white gate, she slowed down in the hope that David would come running down through the woods and shout that the twins were safely home. But they reached the signpost first, and Jenny was still talking when David came toiling up towards them. Peter knew at once by his dejected look that he had had no luck.

"Nobody about except the tall thin chap," he puffed as he reached them and flung himself down in the heather. "He hadn't seen them. They're not there, Peter, and I couldn't find Mrs. Sterling either . . . If I had I think I'd have told her . . . Anyway we'd better get on, and I suppose the best thing to do is to go right up to the top if we don't find a clue first."

So Jenny, rather silent now as she realized that the others were really worried, led the way up the track.

Black Dingle looked very different to David this morning. When he had hurried down it two evenings ago in the rain he had noticed little beyond the fact that it was lonely and rocky. Now, in the sunshine, he could see how wild was this country and how difficult it was going to be to find the twins if they were in hiding or if they were hurt. As they climbed the winding track and jumped the stream which all the time tinkled at their feet, David watched anxiously for any sign that Dickie and Mary had come this way.

Every hundred yards they stopped and whistled and called the "Peewit" cry, and then listened anxiously for an answer.

David said suddenly:

"What are all those black marks on that cliff over there, Jenny? What is that place?"

"I was telling Peter the other day. They're caves I think, or the entrances to the old mines."

"Of course," he replied. "I remember Reuben told us about the mines and how dangerous they were. It would be grand to explore up there one day. What are they like, Jenny?"

"I've never been right up there," she said. "But somewhere over on the left there are ruins of some miners' cottages. I hate them. They're old and falling to bits and smelly and full of bit-bats."

"There ought to be a track leading over to them. Have we passed it, Jenny?"

"No, but we're nearly there. It's where Peter and me heard that horrible screaming noise that night the mist came"

"I wish I knew what that noise was," Peter said. "I told you about it, David, and you laughed—but you didn't jolly well hear it. You'd have hated it too."

"It was here," Jenny said suddenly. "I remember this hawthorn tree. And this path going off to the left here must be the one that leads to the ruined cottages. This was the place, wasn't it, Peter?"

"Yes—I think it was . . . What are we going to do now, David? Ought we to separate, do you think? Perhaps somebody ought to go up to the top to the Chair? We don't even know if they came this way, do we?"

"Oh, yes, we do," David shouted excitedly. "You bet we do, Peter. We were right! They've been this way. Look!" and he bent down and picked up something small and brown and held it almost reverently in the palm of his hand as the girls jostled him in their eagerness to see the treasure.

"Why," said Jenny, "it's just an old 'conker' with a hole through it."

"That's it," said David. "It's Dickie's 'mastock,' as he calls it. He's had it since last autumn, and it's the most amazing conker in the world. He says it beat the whole school, and I know that he carries it with him wherever he goes. It's the only thing he changes out of his pockets. Haven't you ever seen him with it, Peter?"

Peter shook her head. "No, I haven't, but it sounds like him. What shall we do now, though? Which way shall we go?"

David looked at the ground again and then up at the steep and precipitous sides of the valley over on their left.

"What's that?" he said sharply, and pointed over their heads. "Is this where you heard that odd row in the mist, did you say?"

The girls nodded and then looked up. High above them, stretching right across the sky, were four thin black lines. As their eyes followed David's outstretched hand, they could see that they seemed to reach the cliff face over on their left and disappeared by one of the black openings that Jenny believed to be caves.

"Wires!" said David excitedly. "It's a cable railway, I believe. I expect that's an entrance to a mine over there, and it looks as if the cable takes the cars right across the valley . . . but I can't see where it finishes on the other side, can you?"

"No," said Jenny. "The trees get in the way. That side

of the valley isn't as steep . . . But what was the noise? Wires can't make a noise, and this was *awful* . . . I don't believe it was earthly," she added in an awed whisper.

"I expect it was one of the cable cars rushing across the valley," David said.

Peter looked scared. "But nobody uses the mines. They've been deserted for years, Jenny said. You did say so, didn't you?"

"Of *course* it wasn't a cable car," Jenny replied. "It couldn't have been. Dad told me once that long before I was born the last miner left these parts . . . The noise we heard was a beastly noise, and I think it was one of the Seven Whistlers or something . . . And you needn't ask me to go up to the Chair, because I won't. I'd rather go home and get into trouble there. I'm not going to be left alone, anyway . . ."

David interrupted. "All right," he said briefly and pocketed the conker. "Come on—we'll go over towards those ruined cottages. The mastock was on this path."

After a few minutes they came to a little wood and, once through this, they saw the ruins of the cottages close under the cliff. As Jenny had said, the ruins were unpleasant, but they had to be explored. They called and whistled and pushed their way over the piles of broken stones and nettles, but could find no sign that the twins had been this way. Bats fluttered helplessly as they spoke briefly to each other in an effort to break an eerie silence, and suddenly Jenny said in a choky voice, "I *hate* this place. Come away. It's vile."

The others did not like it either, but David would not leave until he had satisfied himself that there was nothing to find. Most of the cottages had been little more than hovels, but three of them had a room upstairs, and after a meaning look at the stubborn Jenny, who had removed herself to the edge of the clearing, he led the way back to the nearest ruin. In this one half the steep staircase had collapsed, but he jumped for the edge of the top stair and hauled himself up as if he was in the gym. at school. He was sure that he would find nothing, but felt he must now search every square inch that he had missed the first time. But he found only dust and rotting floorboards and the droppings of birds. The second cottage was like the first, and at the third he managed to pull Peter up beside him as a huge grey rat scuttled across the floor. But there was nothing to find—no clues. Not even a 'mastock'. When they came out into the open again he looked at his watch and saw that it was past twelve.

"We'll just go up to the edge of the cliff before we eat," he said. "I can see now where the wires go in. Look! There's a crack in the rock just above what looks like quite a big cave . . . And the path seems to lead there, too. Let's try it. We must go everywhere now we're here."

So they trudged on and the path began to zig-zag as it climbed towards the cliff. After a while it brought them to a little grassy plateau, and for the first time was disclosed an entrance to a big cave which now seemed blocked by an enormous mass of rock. Above this was another hole in the rock face looking rather like a big window, and through this the wires of the cable railway disappeared. David turned to emphasise the discovery, but before he could speak Peter seized his arm and pointed. Coming sedately into the sunshine from the shadowed entrance of the old mine was a small black dog. He was wearing a bow of bright green ribbon round his neck and, at the sound of voices, he stopped, cocked his head and lifted one paw.

"It's Mackie!" Peter whispered. "I know it is, and he's wearing Mary's bow. I grumbled at her last night for not taking it off when she went to bed . . . I think they've sent him as a messenger."

8. Moonlight Mystery

THE TWINS had taken no more than six steps away from the shelter of the barn when Dickie pulled at Mary's hand and stopped her. The night was clear and still and the great moon, high over the mountain now, laid a soft sheen of silver over the roofs of the house and patterned the yard with black shadows. All was very quiet, and the very beauty of the night made the silence more intense.

Dickie spoke in a whisper.

"What are we doin' this for, twin? I'll come with you, but I want to know why . . . I just woke up and knew you wanted me like we do sometimes, but it's all rather funny and peculiar."

Mary looked puzzled. "I don't quite know, Dickie. It's old Uncle Micah, and I know he's unhappy and worried, and I saw him from Peter's window upstairs. He came out quietly, but he looks awful and lonely, and I think we ought to see where he goes and help him if we can. Will you, Dickie? Let's just see where he goes."

"All right! It's adventure for us, isn't it? Bet the others will be wild. Serve them right for not waiting to show us H.Q.2 yesterday . . . That click we heard was that gate over there, I'm sure . . . Look! Mackie is waiting for us. Come on."

The white gate was the little wicket leading to a path down through some trees to a rough plank-bridge crossing a stream. They had not yet explored this path and Dickie hesitated again with his hand on the latch.

"Humphrey, or the other one, told me this leads to Black Dingle. D'you think old funny-face has gone this way? I've thought of a name for him, twin. It's Beaver. A chap at school told me that his brother said that once— a long time ago it was, I guess—all men with beards were called Beavers. Seems silly to me, but it's funny . . . Old Uncle Beaver we'll call him . . ."

"Come on," said Mary. "We'd best hurry, Dickie, else we shall lose him."

"An' what are we going to do when we find him?" asked the more practical twin. "Are we going to cheer him up and go along with him?"

"No-o-o! I don't think we'd better let him see us, but we'll just be near in case he wants us."

So they closed the gate softly and went hurrying down through the gloom of the copse to the bridge. Under the trees it was dark and cold, and they were both shivering as they crossed the chattering stream. The path turned uphill to the left and followed the water as it wound round rocks and through thickets until they found themselves in the moonlight again.

"I think this is a short cut to the Dingle, twin," Mary said. "What I call 'our lane' is down there to the left somewhere. Let's stand and listen a moment."

But there was no sound to break the silence, and except for Macbeth, who stood panting slightly between them, they seemed alone in a phantom world of black and silver.

"Phew!" said Dickie suddenly. "It's a bit ghostly, isn't it?"

"There's something white sticking up in front there, Dickie. I've been watching it. It doesn't move. What is it?"

Dickie shivered and jammed his hands into the pockets of his corduroys. He gulped and drew a deep breath before he trusted his voice. Then, "Just an old stick or something," he said. "Never mind about *that*, Mary. What we want is Uncle Beaver, else we'd better go back to bed."

"*Go back?*" said Mary scornfully. "When we're pledged to this great adventure? You're not afraid, are you, twin?"

Dickie's answer was a snort as he started on ahead.

So, in single file, they continued on their way up the track, until they left the trees behind and found themselves in a little valley, at the top of which was the ghostly finger pointing to the sky. And when they reached it they found that it was nothing more than an old weather-beaten sign-post standing in the middle of a little rocky plateau round which their friend the stream now slid sullenly.

"Gosh!" said Dickie. "We've been here. This is the way we came the other day with David and Peter. Don't you remember, Mary? We came down this valley from the Chair. What are we going to do now?"

But Mary was looking at the arm of the signpost.

"You're right, twin. It says 'Black Dingle to Devil's Chair.'"

Then Macbeth barked sharply. He was standing under the signpost with ears cocked and his little square head tilted on one side. He was looking up the Dingle and lifted one paw as Mary bent and put her hand on his collar.

"Quiet, Mackie! What is it, boy?"

He barked again, and there was a scuttling in the heather as a rabbit dashed into the open, jumped the stream and bounded up the path. Macbeth yelped madly, broke from Mary's restraining hold and bolted in pursuit. She called him in vain, but Dickie was not really listening. He was pointing up the Dingle and squealing with excitement.

"I've seen him! Look, Mary! I'm sure that's old Uncle Beaver . . . Wait, and you'll see him, too."

Higher up the valley, perhaps a quarter of a mile ahead, the path left the stream and passed over a high rock. This rock was easily seen in the moonlight and, as the children watched, a thin black figure climbed slowly up and for a long moment was silhouetted clearly against the sky.

"Come on," said Mary. "That's him. We must follow him, Dickie . . . Somebody has got to look after him, else he'll do something awful."

So without further words they left the plateau and started up the forbidding valley. Macbeth gave up the unequal chase—his legs were much too short for rabbit-catching—and trotted sedately at Mary's heels, but although they went as fast as they could, they did not see Uncle Micah again until they, in turn, reached the rock. From the top they could see far up the valley and could see, too, the shape of the black rocks of the Devil's Chair looming high over the wild countryside. To their left towered the steep cliff-like sides of the Dingle, gleaming brightly in the moonlight. As they paused, tired now and rather breathless, Mary pointed ahead, and for a brief moment they glimpsed the fugitive crossing a path of turf farther up the valley. He was walking steadily and rather mechanically, and, as far as they could see, he looked neither to right nor to left.

"Gosh!" said Dickie. "He's in a hurry, twin. Looks as if he's going right up to the Chair. Bags we don't go up there."

"Pooh!" answered Mary. "I'm not afraid of that old Chair. You know we're not, Dickie! . . . But I do want to know where he's going."

"Yes, twin. I do, too. I always want to know things. I think maybe he's got a secret in his life."

"Yes, Dickie. A dark secret, too. And his heart is breaking. I know it is, Dickie, and we've got to help him. Nobody else can help him, I believe, 'cept us."

"All right, Mary, only I don't feel like that at all. I think really that he's a silly, grumpy old man, and I don't know why we've got to see where he goes . . . and I'm jolly hungry," he added inconsequently.

Mary looked shocked, but said nothing. This was one of the times when Dickie accepted her leadership without question, and she knew that although he would not admit it, he would now rather be back in his sleeping-bag at H.Q. 2. Just for a moment, she, too, felt a sharp pang at the remembrance of Peter's sleeping face in the moonlight as she had seen it a few hours before, but, for some odd and unexplained reason, she felt that she had a job to do, and that she would not turn back until this mystery of Uncle Micah had been solved.

So without a word—and largely because she did not quite trust herself to speak with a steady voice—she led the way down the farther side of the rock till the track ran by the stream again.

Now the wind strengthened and they could hear it moaning among the rocks up by the Chair. It suddenly got darker.

They had reached a grassy level where three paths met—the place where they had seen Uncle Micah from the top of the rock—when Mary suddenly realized how silly they were. She was cold and tired. No longer did she feel a leader, and all she longed for was her sleeping-bag at Seven Gates, or, better still, her cosy little bed at Witchend. There was no sign of Uncle Micah and no indication of the direction in which he had gone, although she seemed to remember that he had crossed this little oasis and gone straight up towards the Chair. She looked at Dickie and unexpectedly felt for his hand. He knew what she was thinking without words.

"All right, twin. Let's go back now. We'll never find the silly old man now, and it doesn't really matter, does it? . . . Let's just rest here a minute, 'cos I'm jolly tired, and then we'll go straight back an' just slip in quietly and not say a word till breakfast-time."

Just then the moon came out from behind a cloud and the night was made day again.

"I don't like this place any longer," Mary said suddenly. "I hate it, Dickie. Let's go. If I wasn't so tired we'd run."

"Sssshh!" Dickie interrupted suddenly. "Listen, Mary. I heard something."

They stood stock still, but only the wind moaned among the rocks and the stream gurgled and sang at their feet on its way down the valley.

Dickie's voice was shaking when he spoke again.

"Voices," he whispered. "Someone talking, far away. Listen, Mary, and tell me if *you* can hear . . . Mary, I *did* hear something. True I did . . . *Keep still, Mackie, and don't pant, you silly little dog* . . . Oh, gosh! Mary, I do hate this beastly place. Let's go now."

But almost before he had finished speaking Mary grabbed his arm so fiercely that he winced and shook himself free. She was pointing up towards the cliff on their left.

"Look, twin, I can see them. Look! *Oh, Dickie, I hate it!* Let's go."

But then, at that very instant, the moon was covered again and it was as if a veil had been drawn over a picture of the high cliff-tops and the woods below them. Where, a second before, all had been sharp in the clear, cold light of the moon, now all was hazy and indistinct. But as Dickie strained his eyes to follow Mary's shaking finger, it did seem as if tiny, shadowy figures moved across the skyline. Not one figure. Not Uncle Micah's lonely silhouette, but an uncanny, silent procession of shapes that might have been men or beasts or both.

Now it was Mary who weakened. She gave a little wail of fear and covered her face in her hands.

"Dickie!" she cried. "Dickie! Did you see them? It's the ghost-hunt that Peter and Jenny told about. Edric was the Black Huntsman's name, and behind him rides the fair Godda, his bride on a white horse. Hide, Dickie! Let's hide! Don't let them see us," and she cowered down on the grass in terror.

Now it was just then that because his beloved twin was tired and frightened that Dickie felt strong and brave again, but before he could answer and comfort her a rabbit jumped out almost at their feet and bounded away up the track on their left, which led towards the cliffs. This was too much for Macbeth, who with one yelp dashed madly in pursuit. Mary straightened and wiped her eyes. She was already ashamed of her outburst.

"He's a very naughty, disobedient little dog," she said, and began to call and whistle to him. Dickie joined in, but several minutes passed as it grew quickly darker, and Macbeth did not return. A startled owl drifted silently over their heads and then called loud and clear as he swung up out of sight above the treetops. The children's cries and whistles came back to them faint and mocking as ghostly echoes, and that was all.

Then Mary started to run up the path.

"Where are you going, Mary? We're going home, aren't we? That's not the way."

She turned on him like a little fury.

"What a selfish beast you are, Dickie. Do you mean you'd go home *and leave Mackie all alone and lost up here in this beastly place?* It's horrid of you, Dickie . . . I believe I almost hate you."

"Oh, ALL RIGHT," Dickie answered. "I don't really want to leave him, and you know I wouldn't, but I want to go home and so do you, and it's getting cold and dark, and he'll follow us like he always does."

"Sorry, Dickie," she answered. "I'm sorry I said I nearly hate you. I don't . . . But I won't leave him alone in this awful, ghostly valley . . . Come on . . . We'll soon find him."

Dickie fumbled in his pocket.

"All right," he said. "An' just wait till we catch him! He's a naughty little dog. I've got a piece of string here somewhere, and when I get him he's jolly well going to be tied up, and I'll lead him like that all the way home." .

Mary stood by while he produced an astonishing collection of old junk and turned it over with loving fingers. He found the string and disentangled it as best he could, but neither of them noticed the old "mastock" conker fall to the ground.

Then together they started off down the new path, farther from home and farther even from the road they knew. They whistled and called frantically till their lips and voices ached. Once, very far ahead, they heard Mackie bark, and so they pressed on in the dark, forgetting how tired they were, forgetting how long it would take them to get back, forgetting everything except that their beloved Macbeth was somewhere ahead chasing something which he would never catch and that they could not go back without him.

Soon the path broadened and led them through a wood. Once out of the shadows of the whispering trees they were startled by some big, rugged shadows. Dickie stopped abruptly.

"What are they, twin?"

They advanced slowly, hand in hand. The shadows did not move, so they went nearer. Then the moon came out again and they saw the ruined cottages.

"They're horrid!" said Mary with a shudder. "They look dead."

They whistled again and called in vain, and so, rather despairingly now, and with lagging steps, they trudged on up the track, which had now broadened into a lane. Twice they heard Macbeth yelp excitedly in front of them; twice they hurried on as the road climbed steeply, and twice they were disappointed when they turned a corner.

But at last they reached journey's end and saw before them the towering cliffs that now barred their way. They could go no farther. The road just disappeared under their feet, and they found themselves on a grassy plateau with the dingle at their backs and the entrance to a dark cave in front of them. Before the cave was Macbeth, with his head on one side and one paw lifted as he listened. At the sound of the twins' voices he wagged his tail, but did not turn. Mary called him sharply again. He whined and barked, but did not move.

"He can hear something," said Dickie. "Come on."

The moon came out again as they crossed the grass, and, at the same instant, they both heard the distant murmur of men's voices. Dickie felt Mary's hand shake in his, and, although he could feel his own heart thumping in fear, he went bravely forward.

At the sound of the voices, the dog barked again and dashed ahead into the dark entrance of the cave.

The children went closer and saw at once that it was not quite an ordinary cave, but more like the entrance to a mine which was partly blocked with stones and rocks.

Mary stepped cautiously forward.

"Look, Dickie! Some of the stones are loose. They've fallen from somewhere, but I can squeeze in. Mackie, come here at once! And here's a whopping big rock, Dickie. DICKIE! IT MOVED! Of course it did, you chump! Come and try for yourself. I TELL YOU IT MOVED! . . . I don't like this place either. Come out, Mackie, you naughty, naughty dog!"

The moon was shining full into the choked entrance now, but they could not see far inside. Even as Dickie came in out of the moonlight it seemed from somewhere there came again the mysterious sound of phantom voices. Macbeth barked and whined in the darkness, and then rushed excitedly back to the children. Mary grabbed at him, but Dickie was feeling the rock that moved.

"It's peculiar, Mary, but it *does* move. You're right. What a funny great stone. P'raps it's balanced on something like the stone doors that used to guard treasure and only moved when you said the magic word. Let's try a word . . . Open, SESAME! No good! I didn't think that would do. Oh, gosh, Mary! It's moving a lot. Feel! GOSH! IT ROCKS! It's rocking now . . . Let's give it a real push! . . ."

They both pushed and pushed too hard. There was an ear-splitting crash as the balancing rock swayed and then fell sideways across the entrance.

Except for a few fugitive gleams, the cave was now dark and the way out was barred.

Mary cried, "What have we done?" and Dickie, "Gosh! that surprised us, didn't it? 'Spect that was a trap really." But his voice broke on the last sentence, and only once before did he remember being so frightened. Macbeth whined at their feet and the twins clutched each other as the silence, like the darkness, closed round them.

E

9. The Cable

Macbeth's sudden appearance at the entrance of the mine affected Peter, David and Jenny very differently. Peter was the first to see him. "It's Mackie!" she whispered. "I know it is and he's wearing Mary's bow. I grumbled at her last night for not taking it off when she went to bed . . . *I think they've sent him as a messenger.*"

Jenny squealed excitedly, "He must be haunted. He's come from nowhere," but David called quietly, "Come here, Mackie."

The little dog watched them with interest and slowly wagged his tail. David called him again, and rather condescendingly he ambled over, jumped up to lick David's bare knee, and then rolled on his back to have his chest tickled.

"It's Mac right enough," said David, as he accepted the dog's invitation. "Are you sure about the ribbon, Peter?"

"Yes, of course I am. I know Mary was wearing it when she went to bed, and this proves that Mackie has been with them. They must be somewhere near . . ."

"Let's call them," said Jenny. "Let's shout and shout!"

But David was looking fixedly at the cliff face, and the opening above where the wires of the railway cable disappeared. Then he ran over to the rocks below, went down on his knees and peered into the narrow opening.

"Mackie might have come through here," he called excitedly. "It looks as if there's a narrow tunnel through these rocks, but it's not big enough for the twins. You saw him first, didn't you, Peter? Did he actually come out of this tunnel?"

Peter shook her head. "I don't know. He just seemed

to come from behind that big rock in the shadow . . . Let me look."

Then Jenny flopped down beside them and David found his torch and shone it into the dark opening. But there was nothing to be seen, as other rocks seemed to block the narrow passage after a few feet.

They all called and whistled the Peewit cry again, but only haunting echoes came back from the rocky cliff above them.

David sat back on his heels.

"I believe he came out of that hole," he said stubbornly and tried to lift some of the rocks that blocked the way in. But they were too heavy for them to shift, and after they had all strained and pulled for a few minutes, David said: "We're wasting time and being silly chumps as well. Let's sit down sensibly and talk it over. We've got to decide quickly what's the best thing to do. What d'you think, Peter?"

"I'm worried, David. You know I am. I keep on remembering that dream about Mary and I think that p'raps something has happened to them. I vote we go straight back and tell the grown-ups. I think we ought to do that now because we can't search all the hills ourselves and they ought to get a proper search party out . . . I'm sorry, David, but that's what I think."

David rolled over and grunted.

"What about you, Jenny?"

Quite flustered at being asked for an opinon, Jenny didn't seem to know what she did think.

"Thank you very much for asking me, David," she began, "but I believe I ought to be going home now. I'd forgotten I'd run away again and I'll get into awful trouble about it this time . . . Yes, I think Peter's right. We'd better go at once 'cos we can't do anything here."

David made no answer but called Macbeth and offered him a piece of sandwich from the knapsack. The dog accepted it out of courtesy, but could not be bothered to eat it.

"Funny," mused David. "He's not hungry and he's not

very worried." He sat up suddenly. "No. You girls are wrong, and although I agree that we ought to tell the grown-ups, I don't think we all ought to go back to Seven Gates. I believe those kids are round here somewhere, and if we all go rushing back we may miss them again. . . . Pity you can't tell us what you know, Mackie. Did Mary tie that ribbon on you . . . ?"

David went on, "You two girls go back and find Mrs. Sterling and she'll tell you what else to do and who else to fetch. I still believe Mackie came out of the mountain."

They packed up rather silently but when they were ready to start down the track, Macbeth refused to come with them.

David looked more worried than ever. "I believe they're about here somewhere. Let's call again."

After they had called and whistled till their throats ached, he said suddenly: "No, this is no good. Do you mind, Peter, if I go with Jenny? I've got some ideas and it will be easier I think if I go down myself. D'you mind staying and keeping a look out? P'raps if you get up really high somewhere you could watch the whole Dingle. Take Mackie with you—you'll have to lead him and I think I've got some string—and he'll be company for you. I'd try to get up to the Chair, if I were you, because you can see for miles from there . . . You'd better take what's left of the grub, too in case you find Dickie—he's sure to be hungry."

"Of course I will, David. Maybe that plan is best, and I think I'd rather you went and arranged the search party. I'll go up to the Chair and if I haven't found them I shall see you when you come back up the Dingle, and I'll come and meet you."

So they tied a length of string round the collar of a reluctant Macbeth and led him protesting down the path towards the ruined cottages.

When they came to the place where David had found Dickie's "mastock", Peter said "Good-bye" to the others who hurried down the path with nothing more from David than: "Keep a good look out, Peter. If they're at home I'll come back right away for you. It's just on two o'clock now, so by four or soon after you can expect us back again. 'Bye, Peter."

Jenny looked thoroughly unhappy. "Hope you don't really mind me going back, Peter," she said, "but I reckon she'll be rampaging all round Barton by now . . . and Peter . . . I wouldn't stay up by the Chair if I were you. Honest, I wouldn't, Peter. Nobody stays up there even in daylight. Please don't, Peter. Keep a good look out from somewhere else."

Peter smiled wanly, patted the dejected Macbeth, and called back:

"Don't worry about me, Jenny—I'll be careful and look after myself, but thanks all the same. Cheerio, David! Why do you have twins that are always getting lost?" And then she turned up the hill towards the black rocks of the Devil's Chair looming terrific over the lonely valley. In a very few minutes the others were out of sight and, as she plodded on beside the stream, she felt the lonliness even more strongly than when she and Jenny had heard the rushing of the cable car in the mist. Peter was a sensible girl and she was used to the solitude of the hills, but there was really something about the Stiperstones and Black Dingle that made her feel uncomfortable and lonely. Really she would have liked to have gone back to Seven Gates with the others, but she did realize that David's suggestion was sensible, and not for anything would she have failed him when he had asked her to do something.

She stopped and looked round again very carefully. She had climbed some distance since leaving the others and was a little out of breath and very hot. Mackie, with tail down, walked disconsolately into the stream and lapped, and Peter bent to pat him. Then she sat down, too, and taking the green ribbon from his collar, fixed it in her own hair and tried to see the effect in a pool. The flies buzzed ceaselessly in the hazy heat. No birds called, and over the desolate scene brooded the black rocks of the Chair.

The path climbed steeply and the loose stones were a nuisance. The stream, smaller now that it was nearer its source, was soon left behind. A few more steps and she reached the plateau at the top of the valley. Above her, the black rocks of the Chair seemed to burst out of the ground and tower dominatingly over all. Both to her left and right the path stretched along the ridge of the mountain, and she could see for miles in every direction. As David had said, the whole Dingle was now below her. She could see that other wild valleys like Black Dingle swung away from the mountain's ridge, and suddenly she realized that if the twins were hurt or even wandering about this countryside, it would be impossible to find them without several skilled search parties.

All was uncannily still, so she sat down with her back to the rocks. Then she must have dozed a little, because afterwards, when she tried to remember, she was not sure how many times Macbeth had growled and whimpered, or whether she really did hear the sound of distant shouting, and once the dull thud of a faraway explosion. She began to think of all the tales and mysteries she had heard about the Chair. She was just wondering whether she was falling under the uncanny influence of the place herself when Macbeth barked sharply and warningly again and again.

She looked down. Below her, like a pale thread in a green and purple carpet, wound the track down Black Dingle. She followed it down with her eyes until she thought she could pick out the cross roads where she had parted from David and Jenny. On her right was the rocky ridge with the closed entrance to the mine. She could not see the latter, but a splash of green she imagined must be the tree tops of the wood by the ruined cottages. She moved a little farther round the rock, but still could see nothing suspicious there and no sign of movement.

Macbeth barked again urgently, as if trying to tell her something. He was facing in the opposite direction so she turned to the left towards the wooded ridge on the other side of the Dingle. Even as she strained to see if there was anything unusual in this direction, Peter realized that, oddly enough, they had never explored this side, or knew much about it beyond the fact that the slopes from the valley itself were not so precipitous and were fairly heavily wooded. She realized too that somewhere above those tree tops must stretch the wire of the cable railway, and wondered where the wires ended.

Then she saw what had excited Macbeth. On the ridge against the skyline, there was the flash of something bright—just as if someone had caught the sun in a mirror. The flash was not repeated but with the light behind her it did seem as if she could see something moving on the ridge. It may have been imagination but it was the first hint she had had of anything alive within miles; so, without further thought, Peter scrambled down the black rocks, called Macbeth, and started quickly along the mountain path.

Just as soon as they had left the rocks of the Chair behind them, they both felt better. She let Macbeth off the string. A refreshing little breeze sprang up and suddenly the day seemed brighter and she laughed aloud in relief to be doing something definite instead of waiting in the gloomy shadow of the Chair.

Then she saw the flash again, but this time it seemed much farther away. Macbeth was waiting for her at a junction of two paths which here crossed each other at right angles, and Peter saw that she had now reached the unexplored ridge which was the northern side of the Dingle, and that the mysterious flashes must have come from the path that ran along its crest.

She turned along it without hesitation, and Macbeth gambolled beside her.

There were no marks of small feet in the dust on the path and the only defined track was that of a bicycle. She looked again carefully and noticed the mark of one tyre only which seemed odd, until she realized that the other tyre must be flat and responsible for the wavy, blurred track which sometimes crossed the line of the hard tyre.

"Come here, Macbeth," she called. "I've been clever. Someone is pushing a bike with a big puncture along here in front of us. I should think those flashes were the sun on the handle-bars. What do you think, Mackie? . . . So do I . . . No. I'm 'fraid it's not the twins, but whoever it is may have seen them. Let's catch him up and see."

But all the same she was not sure if this was the right thing to do. She had no watch, but by the sun guessed it to be nearly four, and that David and his party would be coming up the Dingle soon and expecting to meet her. She looked down into the valley and found that she could still see the cross roads where they had found the conker; but it was obviously going to be very difficult to get down, for there was no sign of a path and the hillsides above the woods were steep and rough. She hesitated, wondering what was the sensible thing to do. She wished David could decide for her—not because she was unused to making up her own mind, but because she was beginning to rely upon his decisions in all their adventures. Should she forget the cyclist—who doubtless was miles away by now—and get down into the Dingle as quickly as possible to meet the others, or should she hurry on, catch the stranger and ask if he had seen the twins? She was just thinking that she ought to do the latter when the problem was solved for her.

She had not realized that, as she was standing bare-headed in the sunshine in a bright blue shirt with not even a bush or a tree near, she must be visible from a very considerable distance, and that although she might not be able to see the stranger in the haze ahead, he might have seen her! Macbeth barked sharply, and now when she looked up she saw a tiny figure far ahead. As she watched it seemed that the figure was coming back towards her, but whether or not it was the cyclist she could not tell, as there were no more flashes.

Then it looked as if the stranger waved, but when a wandering breeze brought with it the faint and plaintive call of the Peewit, Peter's doubt became a certainty.

It was Tom Ingles! Good old Tom, with his honest, cheeky, sunburned face grinning delightedly as he ran forward the last few yards and then stopped rather shyly as they met.

Peter was so thrilled that she nearly kissed him. Just in time she realized that he might not appreciate it, so she held out her hands instead.

"Tom! I never guessed it might be you and I'm so glad to see you."

"It was your blue shirt made me think it might be you, Peter. Dunno what made me turn round and look, I'm sure, but I was fed up shoving that bike along. Where are the others, anyway, and where am I?"

"But I thought it was tomorrow you were coming. That's what we said, didn't we?"

"Yes, you did. But Uncle's been a sport and given me today off, and golly, Peter! it's a gruelling ride all right in this heat. So I decided to come today, and I sent a telegram to Seven Gates saying I was on the way. I got along fairly well, and knew I was well on the trail when I came to a pub called the 'Hope Anchor' down the other side there. The woman there had seen the twins all right. . . ."

"Not today, Tom? She hasn't seen them today, has she?" she interrupted so urgently that Tom looked up in surprise.

"No," he said wonderingly. "Why?"

"I'll tell you in a minute. Go on. Tell me how you got here and then I'll tell you our adventure . . . We've lost the twins again, Tom."

"Honest? Gosh! That's grim. What can we do? . . . Oh, all right, but I haven't got much to tell. I just got fed up and lost myself twice and had to push the old bike up that mountain. The path was all stones and I got a whopping puncture that made things worse, but I guess I knew Dickie's Devil's Chair when I saw it up there. I didn't know which way to go then, or where I was, but this seemed as good a way as any . . . I say, Peter . . . I've come across a jolly rum place along here. I left the bike there when I saw you, so you'd better come along, too . . . Now buck up and tell me 'bout yourself and those twins."

As they hurried along the ridge, Peter told Tom as quickly as she could of their adventures.

"And you didn't see a sign of them anywhere, Tom? Or anybody to ask? . . . I didn't really suppose that you would, and as I haven't seen them I think the best thing we can do is to get down into the Dingle when we've got your bike and join up with the others . . . I say, Tom! What's that?"

"That's what I want to know. That's the place I told you about. It's a rum show, isn't it?"

"But what's it doing up here, Tom? It looks as if it might be a pump-house. Look! There's a chimney. And what's that sort of chute leading over the edge that side? I say, Tom! I've got it. I know what it is! Remember I told you just now that the place where we found Mackie looked as if it had once been the entrance to one of the old mines and about the cable railway? . . . Well, I bet this is the engine-house and that the wires of the cable finish here. I was wondering where they went."

They hurried on and soon found Peter to be right. The derelict building was perched on the side of the ridge— rather like a medieval castle on the top of a rock—with a squat, square tower facing the Dingle. From one opening in the tower stretched the wires of the cable railway and, on the other side, a wide, iron trough bridged the track on which they were standing. Tom ran across and looked over the edge.

"See here, Peter! There's a wooden chute running down the side of the mountain. Come and look! I've seen one of these before over Ludlow way. They used it to slide tree trunks down into the valley."

Peter joined him and was surprised to see how steep was this side of the ridge.

"This is thrilling, Tom. We must all come here and

explore. We could spend a whole day here . . . I think I see what happened. They mined the ore the other side of the Dingle where we were this morning and then it was hauled across the valley on the cable. Then, I expect, the trucks were emptied into that chute thing up there and the ore went tumbling down into that valley where there's a road or a railway. Let's see if we can get inside."

The engine-house looked as if it had been neglected for years. The trees and undergrowth and nettles grew close to the walls and a dilapidated door hung dejectedly on one hinge. Tom pushed it gently and it uttered a plaintive squeak and moved under his hand. They stepped over the threshold and paused until their eyes became accustomed to the gloom. Then they saw an iron-floored gallery above them—rather like the iron floor of a pier—and the bulk of a mighty drum and some machinery. On their left, in the shadows, a dark cyclinder towered up into the roof.

"Bet that's a steam-engine," Tom said. "But I wonder where they got the water? Reckon they'd have to pump from down below somewhere . . . There's a ladder here, Peter. Let's explore up top."

Up on the gallery they saw how the engine had been used to wind the cable on to the drum and then they saw the actual cable car—a big, round iron container, with two steps or ledges on the outside large enough for a man to stand upon. The whole was suspended by a rather complicated pulley block upon which were two short levers.

Tom climbed to the steps and reached up to the pulley block. "Reckon those are brakes," he said. "Looks as if you could ride over the valley on this thing holding on to those handles on the edge."

But Peter was not listening. She had squeezed past the iron car and was standing on the edge of the platform looking out of the opening over the Dingle.

"Just look here, Tom," she called. "I can see *everything*."

The car swayed and creaked on its chains as Tom jumped off and went over to her side. Together they knelt

down and peered cautiously over the edge to see the tree
tops far below them, and the side of the valley dropping
almost sheer for a hundred feet. Peter drew back a little
and gasped, "It's deep, isn't it? Look at the wires, Tom.
You can see how they stretch right across . . . And look
again . . . Do you see that little black dot in the cliff the
other side? That's where the wires go in, and just below
is where we found Mackie . . . Where is he, by the way?"

They looked round, realizing that they had forgotten the
dog in the excitement of exploration, and then whistled
for him. Peter was relieved when he gave an answering
yelp from below.

"Of course, he can't climb the ladder," she said. "Can
you see him through the floor, Tom? What's he doing?"

Tom peered through the iron grille of the platform.

"He's eating something down in the corner there," he
said. "We'd better stop him. You know what a little
scavenger he is. I'll fetch him."

He clattered down the ladder and then called excitedly:
"I say, Peter, he's eating biscuits out of a paper bag.
Someone's been here lately. I can see footsteps in the
dust now round this boiler . . . and there's some oil been
dropped here from just under the drum . . . I reckon this
place is being used after all . . . And here's a bit of candle,
too . . ."

But before he could say any more Peter called excitedly
from over his head:

"Come quickly, Tom! David and the others are coming
up the valley! He's got some men with him. It's the search
party . . ."

Tom tucked Macbeth under his arm and climbed the
ladder again to her side.

The shadows were lengthening a little now, and a chilly
breeze stirred the tree tops as a reminder that summer was
still some months ahead. Far over the other side of the
Dingle, past the patch of trees by the ruined cottages where
the track began to climb up to the entrance of the mine,
Tom could now see the tiny figures of the rescue party.

"You can't see the track till it comes out of the wood by the miners' cottages," Peter explained. "That's why we didn't see them at first. They must have come up the valley while we were exploring downstairs . . . Look! David's brought Sally, and I think that's Jenny, and there are some men, too. . . . Oh, Tom! I do feel a pig. I promised to be there, and now David will be worrying 'bout me, too. What shall we do?"

Tom looked back slowly at the cable car. When he turned to her again his eyes were bright with excitement.

"Are you game, Peter? Shall we chance it? I'll go on my own if you like. I reckon I could work the thing. I believe the car runs back on its own from here when it's empty, 'cos we're higher than the mine on the other side, and then the engine pulls it back when it's full by winding up the wire on the drum. All we have to do is to let off the brake and then tighten it again when we get to the other end . . . Shall we risk it, Peter? We'll be there before them if we start now."

Peter looked at him in admiration. This was a Tom she had not met before, but perhaps this was because when they were all together he had generally been ready to let David take the lead.

He grinned. "It'll be like the pictures. Come on, Peter. Let's go."

"What about your bike?" Peter suggested with a thumping heart and rather a shaky voice.

"I'll come back for that one day. It's no use with a flat tyre, anyway. Come on. Put Mackie in first and then you hop in. I'm going to stand on the step here and hold on to these handle things."

So, protesting and unhappy, Macbeth was dropped into the big bucket, and then Tom hoisted Peter up until she could get a leg over the edge.

"Right away, guard!" he called, and reached up to the little handle on the pulley block. The car swayed, but did not move, so, holding on with both hands, he put out one foot and pushed.

Peter, with her head just reaching over the edge of the car, saw the platform moving backwards, and then suddenly they were out in the evening sunshine. She glanced at Tom's exultant face a few inches from her own, and then looked down, and was only just able to check an involuntary scream. Deep, deep below them the tops of the trees were careering madly backwards and every second the speed of the car increased and the friendly earth seemed farther away. The car swayed violently and the pulley block over her head screeched as the wires tore through it. Macbeth cowered and whimpered at her feet, and she felt sick and dizzy and for a few seconds closed her eyes in terror.

When she opened them again it was to look ahead, and now she did call out as she saw the solid face of the cliff rushing towards them. The tiny black hole through which the cables disappeared was now growing larger every second, and the turned to shout at Tom. But Tom's face was white and glistening as he clung with one hand to the handle on the edge of the car, and with the other fumbled with the lever above him.

Peter saw his lips moving, but could not hear what he was shouting. It seemed like "The brake! Can't fix it . . . Sorry, Peter."

For a second she looked down again and glimpsed white, frightened faces staring, speechless, up at them. She screamed out something as the great jagged black hole in the rock rushed towards them; then she covered her face with her hands and ducked on to the floor of the car as it careered madly into the blackness.

10. *The Handsome Stranger*

T<small>HE SOFT ECHOES</small> of Dickie's whisper, "'Spect that was a trap really," died away in the darkness as Mary clutched at her twin with one hand and felt for Macbeth with the other. Then, "What have we done, Dickie?" she said shakily.

Dickie searched for his courage. Then he said loudly, "Pooh! it's quite all right really, Mary. We just happened to touch that old rock and it tumbled and we'll have to get out a different way . . . Let's just stop still for a minute and try an' find out what to do . . ."

"It's not quite *pitchy* dark, is it, twin? There's some light up there . . ."

They looked up and, sure enough, high above their heads was enough moonlight for them to see a scaffolding or gallery with some ropes and wire stretching away into the dim shadows.

"There's no roof, Dickie. It's hollow," Mary whispered.

From somewhere ahead of them in the darkness came a man's voice.

"Anybody there? Where are you?"

Mary was about to call back, but Dickie sensed what she was going to do and covered her mouth with his hand.

"No," he whispered. "Not yet. It may be a ghost or something who doesn't know we're here . . . 'Sides, I want to see if we can get out," and he turned in the darkness and began to struggle with the fallen stones. Macbeth tried to help him, too, but before Mary could say anything the mysterious voice called again, "Hello, there!" and Macbeth barked sharply.

"It's no good," Dickie said, gulping back a surprising

sob. "It's no use. I can't move the beastly, vile stones. Oh, gosh, Mary, I wish I was bigger . . . Jus' you wait till I'm bigger, and I'll throw old rocks like this about."

Then Mary called back, "Hello, whoever you are. We're here. Will you come and rescue us, please?"

Then they saw the yellow gleam of a torch and heard the sound of running feet.

It was a cheerful young man in a khaki uniform, who stopped in astonishment when the beam of his torch picked out the twins standing hand in hand in front of a pile of fallen rock.

"Great jumping Jehosophat," he drawled. "Look who's here. I'll say it's Hansel and Gretel or the babes in the wood."

"Yes, that's right. We are Hansel and Gretel often," Dickie said.

"But not tonight," Mary added.

"We're footsore and weary," Dickie went on.

"And in need of bread and sup," Mary finished triumphantly.

"Wait! Wait!" was the stranger's reply. "I'll say you are. But what's happened here?"

"Well, you see," Dickie began patiently, "we came in, but we can't get out 'cos the rocks fell down."

"These are the rocks," Mary added politely as she gestured behind her.

The stranger scratched his head. "This shore is a rum country," he said at last. "Tell me, kiddoes, am I dreaming or is it 'bout four o'clock in the morning?"

"We wouldn't know," Mary said sweetly.

"Not having a watch, you see," Dickie added, and then they launched into the familiar formula of introduction.

"I'm Mary Morton, and this is my brother Richard."

"People call me Dickie. We're twins."

"I can see that," the stranger drawled, "but tell me—do kids like you walk about on the hills all night in this country? What are you doing here, anyway?"

"If you could just move those old rocks for us," Dickie

pleaded, "we could go straight home and nobody need worry 'bout us any more."

"And thank you very much for your kindness," Mary added. "Perhaps I can hold the torch for you?"

Meekly the man handed it over and shifted a few of the fallen rocks at Dickie's direction until the huge rocking stone was disclosed.

"No good," he said. "Would take twenty of our bull-dozers and a shot of dynamite to shift it . . . Come on, kids. You come back with me and meet my pard Jake and sit by the fire and enjoy a bite. We'll take care of you and see you get home safe . . . An' bring the little dawg, too."

"We'd like something to eat, thank you," Dickie said. "But you'll 'scuse us asking, but we don't know who you are. An' what are *you* doing here, anyway? . . . Maybe we don't trust you . . ."

"You're wearing uniform," Mary broke in suddenly, "but you're not English."

"You talk like the pictures," Dickie said thoughtfully, and then laughed. "Gosh! I know what you are! You're an American soldier—you're a Yankee Doodle."

"You've said it, kiddo. I'm the U.S. Army, but there's just a few more of us here as well . . . Come and meet the other half."

Then taking the twins by the hand, he led them away into the darkness, with Macbeth trotting sadly at their heels. It was difficult for the children to know where they were going, but as Dickie flashed the torch from side to side it seemed as if they were in a high-walled gallery. For a little they walked uphill and then turning a sharp corner they felt a fresh and pleasant breeze and caught the smell of wood smoke. Next moment they saw the flicker of a fire and another American voice called out:

"What you found, Jerry? What was the thump? Shore sounded like a fall of rock to me."

Then the twins were introduced to Jake, but they were both so sleepy that they could say little more than "Thank you" when their friends poured them out mugs of bitter coffee and broke open a packet of biscuits.

Mary did her best to help Dickie to tell their story, but sleep to her was what food was to him, and as she was nodding most of the time she knew that what they had to tell sounded rather impossible. But Dickie rambled on with his mouth full of biscuit, and Jerry and Jake were very kind and friendly. The little wood fire burned cheerfully, but did not give enough light for them to see where they were, though the echoes suggested that they were still in the cave. Dimly Mary felt Jake's strong arm folding her in a blanket, and then holding her comfortably against his side. Her head slipped sideways against his shoulder and she remembered no more.

Dickie woke first. A rough blanket covered him, and Mary, breathing evenly, was close against him and keeping him warm. He was lying on a heap of bracken and heather which was tickling his knees and a smell of wood smoke and coffee reminded him that he was hungry again. He rolled over on to his back and saw a rocky roof far above him. For a few moments he lay blissfully recalling the adventures of the previous night, and then there came a pleasant frizzling noise and the smell of something tasty in a frying-pan made him sit up. He saw that they were at the back of the cave, and that between them and the entrance the two American soldiers were busy about a camp fire. Beyond them was the sunshine of a new day. At their feet Macbeth slumbered peacefully.

"Wake up, Mary," he thought, and his sister stirred and sat up at his side.

"Hello, Dickie!" she murmured sleepily. "What have we done, and what will the others say? Adventures just seem to happen to us, but I'm afraid David will be rather cross . . . And where are we now?"

Jake looked up from the fire and laughed.

"Awake, kiddoes? There's a bucket o' water outside. I

guess a wash won't hurt you, but breakfast is ready, and we got to be off soon. We're busy today."

They both felt better after they had put their heads in the water, and when they looked round before going back into the cave saw that they were half-way up the side of a strange and wild valley.

"I know," Dickie said suddenly. "We've walked right through the mountain and come out the other side . . . I say, Mary, do you think they're Commandos? They might be, you know . . . Bags they are. I like them both, don't you?"

Mary nodded. "Yes, I do. They're nice. Specially Jake. They're sort of crinkly and ugly, but I like them . . . But, Dickie, have you thought? We must get home quickly, else they'll be worried, and I'm 'fraid there'll be an awful row . . ."

Dickie felt the same, but as there did not seem to be much they could do about it, suggested breakfast instead. It was a splendid and unusual breakfast, with Jake and Jerry obviously keen to hear everything about their adventures. But somehow, in daylight instead of moonlight, Uncle Micah did not seem so mysterious and frightening as he had in the Dingle the night before, or when he had been creeping out of the farmyard down to the little white gate. They did their best, but could not make him sound very alarming.

"An' how far away would you reckon this Seven Gates outfit to be?" drawled Jake, as he rolled a cigarette in slim, brown fingers.

"We don't know 'zactly from here, 'cos we've never been here before, but it's not far."

"How far in a truck?" Jake persisted.

"Truck?" Dickie puzzled. "Truck? . . . Oh, you mean a lorry, I s'pose? . . . Funny how you Yankee Doodles can't speak English like us."

Mary sensed that this was not a very tactful remark, and tried to change the conversation by drawing attention to Macbeth, who, replete with spam, was dozing by the fire.

She rolled him over and tickled his chest in the way he loved.

"Do you have little dogs like this? Isn't he sweet? We've brought him up, and I think I'd die without him," and taking a crumpled piece of green ribbon from her curls she tied it to the little dog's collar.

Then their new friends began to clear up and explained that they would take them down the valley with them and send them home to Seven Gates in a car or truck when they reached the road.

"We shall like that very much," Dickie said. "An' if one of you could manage to spare just a few minutes to come along and see my big brother and Peter and Peter's Aunt and Uncle Beaver and just explain a bit how we happened to be a bit late, that would be very important to us . . ."

"Do you think p'raps you could?" Mary wheedled as Jerry put a fresh piece of chewing gum in his mouth. But before he could answer Dickie was off again and was talking so fast that none of them heard the sound of horses' hooves on the loose stones outside the cave.

"You'd be surprised to see where we're living now. It's all mysterious and utterly surrounded by white gates. There's a ghosty wood and two funny old dwarfs—they're not really dwarfs, of course, but they're ugly and like Snow White's dwarfs—living close by. An' then, of course, there's Uncle Micah himself, and he's really very ghosty indeed, and wanders about and grumps into his beard and talks like a scripture lesson . . . But it's the gates that are so peculiar. How many d'you think there are, pard?" he added to Jerry.

"Seven!" came a strange voice from the mouth of the cave. "Tell me, am I right?"

Jake and Jerry stopped what they were doing and stopped chewing as well. Macbeth sat up and barked. Mary smiled at what she saw and Dickie's mouth dropped open in astonishment.

Outside in the morning sun, sitting motionless on a magnificent horse, was the most handsome man they had ever seen. He was wearing a khaki shirt with a coloured scarf round his neck, beautiful riding breeches and polished riding boots. His black hair was crinkly and so were his brown eyes and the corners of his laughing mouth.

"Am I right?" he repeated. "I bet there are seven. It's my lucky number . . . Anyway, what's going on here? Who are these children?"

He spoke with a slight American accent, and then explained easily enough that he was an American officer who had only arrived in the district the night before, and he had not to report for duty until the next day.

"I liked the look of the morning," he went on, "so I borrowed this grand chap from the farmer where I'm billeted, and thought I'd explore this funny little old country. But what are you kids doing all mixed up with the army? What's the meaning of it?" he added rather sternly to Jerry and Jake, who soon gave him the story of the noise of falling rocks that roused them in the night and of how the twins had been discovered inside the mountain.

"Are you a cowboy?" Dickie asked abruptly. "I always wanted to know one. You look like one."

The handsome stranger laughed and slipped off his horse. "Wait a minute," he said to the children and went into the cave with Jerry and Jake.

"They're whisperin'," observed Dickie gloomily. "I wonder what's goin' to happen to us now? Do you like the new one, Mary?"

"He's beautiful," breathed his twin rapturously, as the newcomer came back and put a hand across their shoulders.

"Look here," he said. "These men are on an army exercise and oughtn't to have taken care of you at all really, and they've got to get along now. Will you trust yourselves to me? I'll take you home soon, and I sure do find your adventures exciting, and I promise I'll look after you."

"If we get into a row—and we're sure to do that,"

Dickie said, "will you help us and tell them we couldn't really help it because of Uncle Beaver? . . ."

"Uncle Beaver?" asked the stranger. "Who's he?"

"Well, he's really Peter's Uncle Micah, but he's peculiar, and Mary thinks he needs looking after, and acksherly all this adventure is about him."

"You see, we want to help him not to be lonely," Mary went on, "but p'raps you'd better not say too much about him. Just tell them we've been puppets of fate!" she finished triumphantly.

"I see," the stranger said with an odd, strained look in his eyes. "Don't worry. I'll come back with you and make everything all right . . . And I'd like to hear some more of your adventures on the way. Will you trust me?"

"Of course," said Mary. "You understand. We like you, don't we, Dickie?"

"Oh, yes, we like you all right, but you don't know the others, and somehow we don't think they're going to be very pleased about us and our adventure, and it's not going to be easy for the one that takes us home," Dickie replied.

Meanwhile Jerry and Jake had packed up their kit, with the exception of a few packages which they insisted upon putting into the twins' pockets.

"Come and see us, dear J's," Mary begged. "And thank you for looking after us. Just ask for Seven Gates and come an' see us . . . Mackie says thank you, too. He likes spam."

"I wish I had more time to ask you things," Dickie said. "I believe you're Commandos acksherly."

Jerry and Jake stood side by side at the mouth of the cave and saluted.

"S'long, youngsters! Be good."

"And I'd stay in bed at night. Just try it for a change."

And as they ambled off down the track a whistle sounded from the heights and even as the twins watched the hillsides came alive with men until the valley was filled with khaki shadows.

The stranger sat down in the sun with his back to a rock and motioned the twins down beside him.

"Say, kids," he began. "Tell me about this house where you're staying. 'Nine Doors,' did you say it was called? And you said something about an old man. Is he still there? Is he well? . . . And his wife? Tell me about her?"

Dickie and Mary managed to catch each other's eye and a meaning look passed between them.

"Well," said Dickie. "We don't know what to tell except that she's very nice to us, but . . ."

"But we don't think she'll be very nice when we get back unless you come with us and 'splain," Mary added. "But we've told you that already."

"I guess I'll be with you when you ride up," the stranger smiled. "I'll make it right for you. Don't worry. Now, tell me again what happened last night."

So again they told their story, missing out the bits that would require awkward explanations and romancing a little too. But they didn't tell the story well, for somehow they both felt a little uneasy. The adventure itself seemed unreal now, and when they looked round at the strange valley and behind them at a hole in the mountain and beside them at a handsome swashbuckling cowboy, they could hardly believe that they were both awake.

Once or twice, Mary had the odd feeling that the stranger knew what they were trying to tell him before they had spoken, and when Dickie was talking about the big stone that rocked, she was astonished to hear their new friend say quietly, almost to himself—"It still rocks, then." Then, sharply, "I mean, how much did it rock?"

"Oh, quite a lot. An' when we both pushed—just to try it, if you know what I mean—it gave a sort of crunch and a groan and over it went, an' there we were."

"And the old man? Where was he? Did you say he was in front of you all the time?"

"Noooo!" Mary said. "Not exactly all the time. Not up here . . . You see we came up this way 'cos Mackie was naughty and ran away . . . We don't know where Uncle Micah went. He was wanderin' and lonely . . . Can we go back now? . . . And what shall we call you?"

The stranger smiled. "Better call me Uncle . . . Just Uncle," he said. "Say! Suppose we could move those rocks that fell. It would be much quicker to get back that way, wouldn't it? Shall we go see?"

Dickie jumped up.

"'Course it would be quicker. Let's try it, but unless you've got some dynamite 'bout you I don't think we could get out. Jerry couldn't."

"We'll have a look, anyway. I'd like to see the place. Come on, Mary. I've got a torch . . . No, the horse will be O.K. We'll leave him. He won't go far and I can catch him later."

So they left the sunshine and set off into the darkness of the mine again with Macbeth trotting in the rear. They passed the still warm ashes of the fire and the pile of bracken and heather on which they had slept so comfortably. Then their new friend switched on the torch and turned into the heart of the mountain. It was very dark and the walls were damp and dripping as they trudged up the slope. They had been too sleepy last night to notice that many smaller galleries branched off each side of their path, and when they turned to the right at the top of the slope they knew by the echo of their voices that the roof was higher. Then Dickie stumbled and fell, and the torch showed he had tripped over half-buried railway lines.

"Gosh," he said. "Wish we could find one of the trucks and have a ride in it. I'd like to see all this railway system 'cos it seems as if there's lines everywhere."

Mary was now firmly attached to the handsome stranger's free hand.

"I can see light ahead," she said. "It's somewhere here that Jerry found us."

Then they turned another corner and found themselves in a huge cave. Daylight was streaming in through an opening in the rock high up in front of them, and they could see, too, the entrance to several other galleries.

Mary looked up. She wasn't sure but she *thought* she heard "Uncle" say to himself, "Looks just the same" before he switched off the torch and pointed above their heads.

"D'you see those great wires coming in through the window? I reckon those are for cable cars. See where that cable runs? And look here. Buckets on an endless chain leading up to the gallery."

"Show me," Dickie demanded. "I want to see."

So then Uncle explained that the ore was probably mined up the various galleries and brought in trucks to this central clearing house to be emptied. Then it seemed that it was lifted in the endless chain to the gallery where the cable car would be waiting to be filled.

"Then what happens?" Dickie asked. "Where does it go?"

"There's an engine-house on the hill the other side of the Dingle," Uncle said, "and the cable stretches right across to there. When the car here is filled the engine winds the cable up and the full car is hauled across. There it is emptied and the ore sent down a chute into the next valley. When the car is empty it rushes back on its own, and I reckon the cable above here runs uphill a good bit so as to check its pace."

Dickie was listening rapturously but Mary was watching him in frank amazement. She released his hand, and stood back and nudged Dickie.

"What I want to know," she said, "is how *you* know all 'bout this? How do you know if you've only just got here from over there?"

Uncle laughed. "You funny kid," he drawled. "P'raps I don't know. P'raps I just dreamt it."

"You're not a spy, are you?" Dickie demanded suddenly. "We know what to do about them. We had some last summer."

"No, young shaver. I'm not a spy . . . Come on. Let's see where the rock fell last night," and he led the way straight to the very spot underneath the window through which the cable passed. It was soon obvious that the fallen rocks could not be moved without blasting or levers but

Uncle, lying flat on the ground, suddenly called, "Say! Bring that little dog here. Looks as if there's just one little tunnel through. I can feel a draught."

So Mary brought Macbeth over and urged him into the narrow opening. Whether it was because he hated the semi-darkness of the cave or because he could smell the open country only a few yards away, they could not tell, but he did go in without much urging, and the last they saw of him was a wagging tail as he nosed through towards freedom. And then Mary, in a panic, wanted him back again, and although they all lay prone and whistled and called through the hole, he did not come back. Mary stood up and brushed the tears from her eyes in a fury.

"That was *your* fault," she raged at the stranger. "It was your silly, stupid idea to make him go in and now he won't come back and I expect he's crushed to an awful death under these rocks . . . Now get us out of here. I'm sick of this place and I want Mackie."

Uncle laughed. "Don't take on like that, kid . . . it's nothing to make such a fuss about . . ."

Then it was Dickie's turn.

"Fuss!" he shouted. "You leave Mary alone and stop laughing. You've got a funny idea of what's funny if you think Mackie being lost is funny. There's nothing funny 'bout you, and Mary and me would prefer it if you'd go away as far as you can and leave us alone. We do things better on our own, anyway. Funny! Pooh! Don't you just think you can come here to England and talk like you are to Mary and me . . ."

Uncle stopped smiling at once and apologised very handsomely. He seemed surprised by the twins' united front. "O.K.," he said when they were friends again, "we'll go back, but first I wonder if we can see Mackie out of the window up there. Here's an old ladder, and if we can get up to that platform I might be able to lift one of you up so that you can look."

Sure enough the ladder just reached the wooden gallery which ran from the window in the rock close against the wall of the cave under the wire cable. When they had climbed up they saw how the buckets on the endless chain would have tipped the ore into the cable car as it stood empty at the platform. Then they went over to the window and Uncle lifted Mary on to his shoulders so that she could see out.

"I can't see down below," she said. "The rock is too thick. There's a big ledge here we could sit on, but I can see up the Dingle. . . . Ooooooo! There's Mackie! The lovely little darling. MACKIE! MACKIE! He can't hear. He's chasing a rabbit . . . I don't mind now he's safe. He'll wait for us, I know. Let's go now."

But Dickie wanted to look and so they found some old buckets and wooden boxes on the platform and piled them up to make steps, so that he could climb up to the ledge instead of being lifted.

"Just like the Lone Pine," Dickie called when he was peering from the look-out. "Gosh, Mary. We've done it again and found something the others will be mad about. Won't it be grand when we bring them here?"

"O.K., youngsters," Uncle called. "We'd best be going now, for I have to get you home. Come on!"

So rather reluctantly the twins climbed down again and followed him slowly through the great cave.

"Have you noticed, twin," Dickie whispered, "that he seems to know a lot of things 'bout this place that we don't know?"

"Yes, I have," Mary answered. "I'm thinking all sorts of things about him. I think I've discovered his dread secret."

But their guide was not behaving as if he had a secret. He was jolly and friendly and was flashing his torch along some of the side galleries.

"Better come back one day and explore these," he said.

Before Dickie could answer Mary tugged at his hand and stopped. At the same time, without words, he had that odd, unexplainable feeling that his twin was warning him and wanted to tell him something. Sometimes they had this feeling for each other, and it was never wrong. So he stopped, too, and said abruptly:

"Stop a minute, Uncle."

The man turned and switched his torch on the two little figures standing below him in the darkness. Dickie looked at his sister.

In a very little voice she said: "I'm sorry, but we can't go any farther. Not Dickie and me can't. I'm afraid to go back this way, and, anyway, I'm going back for Mackie. When he comes through the tunnel he'll be lonely and frightened if I'm not there . . . I'm sorry, Uncle, but you'd better come, too."

And nothing that Uncle could say would shake them. He wheedled and coaxed and was furious in turn, but although they both became a little tearful at his anger they refused to go forward with him.

"And I'll tell you what," Mary suddenly burst out. "You'd better come with us . . . I'm frightened of this place suddenly. I hate it . . . Come on, Dickie. This place is bad. I know it is. If he won't come we'll run in the dark till we get to the big cave and can see."

So they turned and hurried back, and the mystified Uncle followed them. But they had not gone fifty yards in a silence only broken by the echoes of their footsteps and Mary's sobs when there came a curious sound from behind them. First there was the noise of loose stones falling in a series of sharp cracks and rumbles. They were now back in the central cave, and Uncle swung his torch round so that the beam shone up the main gallery. As they watched, a lump of rock fell from the roof and then one side of the gallery seemed to bulge and waver in the beam of the torch. Uncle turned, grabbed a twin with each hand and raced them over to the blocked entrance of the mine, where they stood with their backs to the fallen stones.

Mary called despairingly for Macbeth, and Dickie was just making for the wooden ladder to the gallery when there came a still heavier rumble in the distance. The sound came nearer and nearer and then a rush of dusty air filled the cave.

Uncle wiped his forehead and put his arm round Mary's shoulders. For a long minute there was silence, then he said quietly:

"Say, Mary, why did you want to come back here? Was it really to look for your little dog?"

The little girl looked up at him with a frown.

"I knew something bad was going to happen . . . I feel different now, anyway . . . Whatever it was I'm afraid of has gone. What did happen?"

"I'll tell you what happened," said Dickie tersely. "That old roof has fallen in. That's what happened, and if someone doesn't come soon and dig us out we'll be jolly hungry."

Uncle laughed. "Don't you worry about that. We'll soon get out of this; but I want you both to go up to the gallery and keep a good watch from your special look-out. If you see anybody call and whistle like fun. Will you do that? I'm going back with the torch just to see if Dickie's guess is right."

And with only a little argument the twins climbed up to the platform and watched him walk across the cave till he reached the dark entrance to the gallery. Then he turned and called:

"Don't worry, kids. Chins up and keep a good look-out. I shan't be long and I'd take you along, but it's important for someone to be on guard."

"Good-bye," called Mary faintly and gulped. Then: "You'd better go up to the crow's-nest first, twin. See if there's room for me on the ledge as well."

There was room, and Dickie reached down a hand and pulled her up beside him. And there they sat facing each other in the rocky alcove, looking out over the lonely Dingle now glowing in the afternoon sun. Every few minutes they whistled and called Macbeth, but he was now far away up by the Devil's Chair with Peter. They explored their pockets and found them full of American chocolate, chewing gum and biscuits, and munched contentedly and in gratitude to Jake and Jerry.

"Better not eat it all at once, twin," said Dickie. "We may be starvin' soon if they don't find us or this Uncle man can't find a way out. We got to make it last. I hate making food last."

"I wonder what happened to Uncle Micah," Mary said inconsequently. "I like this adventure quite a bit, but I'm still 'fraid we're going to get a lot of bother from the grown-ups when we get back."

Dickie thoughtfully shifted a wad of gum to the other side of his mouth. He was thinking of what David would would have to say to him. And of what his father would say, too, when he heard about this adventure, and he was not looking forward to it at all. Although not many people would have guessed it, he was tremendously proud of David, and it was not difficult to imagine how angry he would be when they did get home.

It was about half an hour later and they were getting rather frightened because Uncle had not returned, when they heard, faint and far away behind them, a voice calling.

"Hey, kids," it sounded like. "Hey, you twins. Can you come and give me a hand?"

Instantly Dickie scrambled on to the platform.

"It's Uncle. He wants us. Will you stay and look out, Mary, and I'll go and find him."

But Mary refused to be left alone, and Dickie was secretly rather relieved, so together they climbed down the ladder and advanced slowly across the floor of the cave. But they had no torch, and over by the entrance to the galleries it was very dark, so, while they could still see the light from their look-out behind them, they stood and called.

Back came his voice again.

"Are you near, kids? Listen. I've twisted my ankle and can't walk. I'm just by the front corner of the gallery, but the torch is weak now and maybe you can't see it. Watch now and I'll flash it. Watch carefully."

They strained their eyes and suddenly saw a tiny yellow glow in the darkness ahead.

"Keep it on," Dickie yelled. "We can see you. We're coming!"

But Mary had fallen twice and hurt her knee and Dickie had banged his head on the damp wall of the gallery before they reached him; and when they did find him they fell over him.

"Oh, gosh!" Dickie whispered when he had picked himself up. "He's fainted or something. Here we are, Uncle. Wake up! WAKE UP!" and he shook him vigorously.

The torch was out now and had apparently fallen from his fingers, and it was too dark to see him as he lay up against the wall of the gallery. There was no sound but their breathing and the drip of moisture falling from the roof.

Then Mary spoke, and her voice sounded loud and clear.

"We've got to get him out of here somehow, Dickie. We're 'sponsible for him, and we've just got to do it . . . It's specially important, too, because you know who he is, don't you, twin?"

Dickie's face was close against hers in the darkness and she sensed him shaking his head.

"Silly little boy," she teased. "It's Uncle Micah's Charles come home again. I'm sure it is. How else would he know about this place and ask all those questions? . . . Look out! He's moving . . . Don't let him know we know."

In the darkness they felt him move and then he groaned.

"All right, Uncle. Dickie and me are here. Don't worry any more."

He laughed shakily. "Well done, kids . . . Must have passed out for a minute . . . tripped over a loose rock . . ."

After he had rested a little they helped him up and he stood unsteadily on his left foot with one hand on the wall and the other on Dickie's shoulder.

"Now then," he said. "The torch is finished, so we've got

to get back to the cave. Can you see the daylight ahead, Mary?"

"Yes," she said. "It's easier now we're going back . . . And when Dickie's tired you can lean on me."

So they made the journey. And if Dickie's head ached worse than ever, he didn't say anything, and if the blood from Mary's torn knee ran down into her sandal, and if the pain was really bad when Uncle put his weight on her shoulder, she did not cry either. At last, after many checks, they reached the cave and the welcome daylight.

"Now, young Dickie," said Uncle as he let himself down gently by the ladder, "I can't get up there, so you must. Keep a good look-out and call me if you see anyone. Have you got anything to eat, by the way? There's some chocolate in my pocket when you're hungry."

"Your hands are all bloody," Mary said suddenly.

"So they are," he said. "I'll have to clean up in a minute and you can fetch me some water from the pool over there. And what have you done to your knee, young lady?"

"Nothing," said Mary. "Just a scratch, thank you."

"What I want to know," said Dickie suddenly from half-way up the ladder, "is whether all hope has gone?"

"WHAT?" shouted Uncle.

"What I want to know is whether we're prisoners here for ever?" Dickie went on. "An' how long we've got to make our rations last . . . 'cos that's serious."

"What he means," said Mary soberly, "is whether you found a way out the other way or whether the roof has fallen in back there."

"Yes, it has," he said. "And you're grand kids to be so sensible about it. There's no way through back there, and I slipped and twisted this ankle trying to move the stones. And if it hadn't been for Mary refusing to come with me . . ."

"*That's* all right," said Dickie. "I always wanted to know what being buried alive was like, and this is it. It's not so bad as you might think, is it?"

Uncle laughed. "You get up there and keep a good look-out and Mary will help me for a bit."

So while Dickie climbed to the crow's-nest Mary took Uncle's scarf and dipped it in the icy water of the little pool over the entrance to the gallery. And while she was helping him bind the swollen ankle she said suddenly:

"It's no use pretendin' any more. We know who you are. You're Uncle Micah's Charles, aren't you? The one that ran away to America and broke his father's heart. You are, aren't you? Yes, we thought you were Uncle Charles. Now isn't it lucky we found you, 'cos your poor father is pinin' away for you . . . It's no use your wriggling about like that. You just *got* to listen to me, and I tell you he's pining all the time. He walks about these mountains at night and sits in the Devil's Chair and all the people —except us and Aunt Carol—think he's a wizard. Aunt Carol? That's funny! She's your new mother, I s'pose. What fun for you . . . There! That's better for the ankle. Shall we wash the blood away now? I've never been so bloody before. It's squelching in my sandal. What shall we wet so that we can wash it? I don't wear much acksherly. I've only got a vest on under this shirt and I never seem to have a hankie."

"Use mine," suggested Uncle Charles, "or would you like to tear up my shirt?"

"That would be fun," Mary agreed, "but wouldn't it be more sensible if we made it into a signal of distress . . . you know, like a raft? . . ."

Before he could answer Dickie's voice came excitedly from above:

"Come up, Mary. I can hear voices. I can't see anybody yet, but there's somebody coming."

Mary whirled round and put her hands on Uncle Charles' shoulders.

"I knew it!" she squealed. "It's Mackie that's rescued us. I knew he would. Now listen. PROMISE me, Uncle Charles, promise me, please, and SWEAR, too, that you'll do what we say when we're rescued. Don't say who you are till I say. I've made such a lovely plan, so PLEASE don't ask questions, but promise. Will you, darling, DARLING Uncle?"

Dickie was still calling urgently from above, but for once she had no time for her twin. Her urgent little face was a few inches from Charles's, and in her excitement she was trying to shake him.

"Promise me," she urged. "Promise!"

The laughter died out of his eyes and he dropped a kiss on her curls.

"I promise," he whispered. "You're a grand kid, Mary. Now go up with Dickie and shout like fun, and when you can see who it is let me know."

But before she was on the platform the cave was filled with a peculiar humming.

"There's a lot of people coming," Dickie called. Then, "And something's happening to these wires up here. They're moving."

Charles heaved himself to his feet. "Come down," he roared. "Quickly, Dickie! Down here. Right off the platform. And you, Mary."

But Dickie was so excited that he did not seem to hear.

"I'll see who they are in a sec," he called. "I wonder if they've brought a crane?"

"COME DOWN!" Charles shouted as the humming noise increased and the great cable wire over their heads began to vibrate. Mary turned, saw his face and dashed across the platform. She pulled at Dickie's ankle till he overbalanced and fell backwards on to her. Somehow he sensed her fear as they scrambled together down the ladder as the cave was filled with a fearful screeching, and the daylight faded as a mighty shape rattled and screamed through the look-out window and rushed over their heads into the gloom at the back of the cave.

As the impetus of the car was checked by the incline of the cable the din lessened and Mary whispered shakily:

"Did you see, twin?"

"Yes, I did. It was a ghost ridin' on that truck thing like a big pail."

"Whose ghost, twin?"

"Well . . . I *thought* it was Tom's . . . Poor Tom!" Then suddenly he called with a note of panic in his voice: "Tom! Tom! Where are you?"

And as the cable car glided slowly now back towards them, there came from the twilight the signal of the Lone Piners—the mournful but unmistakable cry of the peewit. And this was followed by the sharp and unhappy bark of Macbeth.

11. *The Rescue*

WHILE THE TWINS were inside the mountain and Peter
under the spell of the Devil's Chair and later meeting
Tom, David was getting his rescue party together.

After saying "Good-bye" to Peter he had hurried Jenny
down the Dingle and then found that she wanted to go
straight down to Barton Beach. "But I don't like Seven
Gates, David," she had said when he protested. "None of
us like it, and I think I'd better go straight home now
and get my row over."

But David had insisted. "Another quarter of an hour
won't make any difference, and, anyway, you're a Lone
Piner now, and you've got to do what I say. If the twins
aren't there, it will be your job to go down to Barton as a
messenger, I expect. If they are there, then I shall go back
for Peter, and you can go home, anyway. Do be sensible,
Jenny. You want to help, don't you?"

Jenny gulped and looked up at him striding along by her
side.

"Yes, I do, David," she said. "I s'pose I'll do as you
say," and she shut her eyes as they hurried into the dark
wood.

Mrs. Sterling was waiting at the top gate, and when
she saw David's anxious face she hurried to meet them,
while Uncle Micah, a lonely, menacing figure, stood in
the yard fingering his beard. Jenny gasped when she saw
him, but David gripped her arm and led her forward. He
told his story quickly and clearly, without trying to shift
the blame.

"So you see," he finished, "although we've no clues
except Macbeth and Dickie's conker, I believe there's a
cave in the mountain, and that's where they are."

"Did ye not see the rocking stone?" Uncle Micah boomed suddenly.

David shook his head.

"It guards the entry to the old mine," the old man went on, "but ye can squeeze past it if you know the way. The little ones could do that."

"There's no entrance there now." David was positive, but he turned to Jenny. "Did you see any way they could have got in?"

But now that Jenny was actually in the presence of the wizard and standing in Seven Gates itself, most of her fears seemed to have fled. He was not as bad as she had thought, and even now, when he wheeled on her with blazing eyes, she spoke out bravely.

"No, there wasn't a place. It was all stones except a little hole where the dog must have come through."

Then Uncle Micah seemed to come to life and everything began to happen quickly. Instead of standing about gloomily by himself and glowering at everybody, he took control and forgot to speak like the Old Testament. He called David a good, sensible lad, roared for Humphrey and then sent him hurrying for rope, crowbars, picks and shovels; he asked Mrs. Sterling to pack up some food in a knapsack, and then turned to Jenny almost gently:

"And you, lass? You're from the village? What do they call you?"

"Jenny Harman . . . sir," she nodded.

The old man smiled—and somehow he didn't look so old when he smiled.

"Very well, Jenny Harman, there is special work for you. Run to Barton and tell Joe Hargreave, the constable, what's amiss. Say that I sent you. Say that in an hour we start from here for the old mine because it would seem that the rocking stone has fallen and that the two children may be in the mine. We bring rope and crowbars, but he must fetch what else we may need, and had better send for one of the quarrymen with explosive to join us later . . . Do you know what to say?"

Jenny repeated his message, tossed back her red hair, grinned at David and was away like the wind. And for the first time she ran through the pinewood without noticing it.

By this time Mrs. Sterling had disappeared and Humphrey was muttering to himself in one of the barns.

"God bless us all," he was heard to mutter. "Never have I seen the like this twenty year. Like the old master he is of a sudden. Like he was before young Mr. Charles go away . . . I seen some rope here come Saturday. Where's that there rope? That's that young Henry again. . . . 'Rope,' Master said. 'And crowbars,' he said . . . Oh, dear! Oh dear! What a commotion and all . . ."

Meanwhile, David ran willingly to fetch and saddle Sally and to carry out many other orders. Mrs. Sterling, with a dazed look on her face, came running out with a bulging haversack and insisted upon David and Uncle Micah eating something at once. Then Humphrey appeared looking very harassed and all hung about with strange implements like a Christmas tree, and Sally was loaded with as much as she could carry. David ran back to H.Q.2 for a few oddments, and could not help wishing Tom was with them, and then Aunt Carol was waving at the gate and wishing them "Good luck."

"Good fires and plenty of hot water ready—and soup," were Uncle Micah's final and surprising instructions.

Jenny had done her job well, for just as the main party reached the lane at the foot of the wood, she came toiling up the hill on a bicycle, while behind her—fifty yards behind—pedalled a red and fat policeman with a large satchel on his back. Uncle Micah waited for the constable, and, with David leading Sally in front, the party climbed the Dingle after Jenny and the policeman had left their bicycles by the signpost.

"We ought to see Peter soon," David said. "Look out for her, Jenny. She may have found them after all."

But there was no sign of her, and they did not think to look up to the ridge on their right, where Peter at this moment had just met Tom. Soon the search party turned left and were hidden in the trees. When they had passed the ruined cottages and come into the open again, David waited for Uncle Micah.

"This is the way we came this morning," he said. "And just past this hawthorn—I remember it—is where we saw Mackie coming out from the rocks . . . There! . . . There's no entrance as you see! And no rocking stone, either."

And it was just at that moment when Uncle Micah had stopped and nodded confirmation to the policeman that they first heard the noise of the cable car and looked up to see it rushing towards them.

"I was right, then," was David's first thought. "It *does* work."

"It hasn't run for years," Uncle Micah gasped.

"There's summun in it," the policeman shouted, and summun on t'back."

And then it screamed over their heads and rushed into the black hole in the face of the cliff. Sally, badly frightened, nearly broke away from David, who was shouting, "It was Tom on the back, Tom Ingles. I know it was," as the others stared at him in astonishment.

Uncle Micah stepped forward, put a strong hand on the pony's bridle and quietened her. Then he turned to David.

"There is something strange here. You say you know that lad riding on the back of the car?"

"Yes; it's Tom. Our friend. But where does the car go? Will he be hurt? Can the car come back?"

Uncle Micah shook his head.

"Not unless the old engine other side of Dingle pulls her back. But why was that lad riding her?"

The policeman had removed his helmet and was mopping his forehead. He was beyond words. Nothing like this had ever happened before, and he seemed bewildered as well as out of breath. Then David stepped up to the over-hanging cliff and shouted again and again for Tom. Jenny echoed him, while Mr. Sterling and the policeman went down on their knees and examined the stones blocking the entrance. When no answer came to their calling, David and Jenny turned to help, and then there came from somewhere above their heads the unmistakable voice of Dickie.

"Except that we're high up and they're all low down, it's like that story where a man came stalkin' through the jungle after months and months of weary explorin' . . ."

"Oh, I know, Dickie," Mary interrupted, "and then they came to a place full of black men, except just for the man they were seekin' and said . . ."

"Dr. Livingstone, I presume?"

"All right, David, don't make such faces. We can see you."

"And a jolly long time you've been coming," Dickie went on indignantly. "We were getting worried 'bout you."

David's fury at being addressed so patronizingly quite swamped his relief, and he rushed back to where he could see the twins leaning precariously over the rock ledge and grinning down at the rescue party. Behind them was the cheery face of Tom, who called:

"Gosh, David. That was some trip. Did you see us come over? I thought we were goners, though, for the brakes didn't work, but it stops itself in there somehow and comes rolling back. Say, David, we must all have a go on this tomorrow. It beats anything on the pictures."

But before any of the rescuers could answer, the twins started again.

"Hello, old Uncle Micah!" Mary called cheekily. "We want to see you very badly. We've got a lot of things to ask you."

"Jus' look what they've brought for us, twin," said Dickie. "It's a policeman. A *real* policeman."

An unmistakable snort came from the representative of the law, but it was Jenny who asked the sensible question:

"How did you two get in there?"

The twins looked at each other and David took the opportunity to speak again.

"Are you all right, Tom? And are those kids all right? And have any of you seen Peter?"

Tom pulled the twins back by the seats of their shorts and leaned forward.

"We're all O.K. as far as I can see. Peter's here, too, wanting to have a word, but from what they tell me they can't get out of here 'cos the mine is blocked up the front as well as the back. You'll have to chuck up a rope to us here, I reckon. *All right, Peter.* Give me a chance."

And then Tom was pulled back and Peter's fair head took his place.

"Well, we've found them, David, and they're all right except Dickie says he's hungry. And they've got the most terrific surprise—*all right, Mary, you little beast, don't pinch!* Do you know what we did? We were over on the other side and I could see you all coming up the Dingle, and Tom said . . ."

"WILL YOU CHILDREN BE SILENT?" suddenly roared Uncle Micah in his old manner. "HAVE YE NO RESPECT FOR YOUR ELDERS? . . . Humphrey, ye great goop! bring me that rope."

Then the constable sat down with his back to the cliff and mopped himself, while Humphrey, still flustered and flabbergasted at the change in his master, dropped the pickaxe he was carrying and then got Jenny mixed up in the rope. When they were disentangled, Uncle Micah showed him that the rope must somehow be thrown over the heavy cable before anything could be hauled up or anybody let down. But this proved more difficult than it looked. The cable was too high and the rope too thin. They tried tying the crowbar to one end and throwing it up that way, but, except that Mary was nearly beheaded as she leaned out offering encouraging remarks, this was also unsuccessful. Then Dickie called out: "Just you wait. We've got an idea. We're going to send a message," and then they both disappeared, and the rescue party sat down for a rest.

By now Uncle Micah was looking very fierce, and David

rather felt he was about to relapse into scripture again. Then came an odd snuffling behind them, and when they looked down it was to see Macbeth emerging for the second time from the little tunnel through the fallen rocks.

"Gosh!" David shouted. "I'd forgotten all about you, Mackie. Where have you been?"

Mackie, looking rather rakish with a green bow and now a white bow in his collar, leapt upon his big master and embraced him. Then he saw the policeman and barked menacingly. He hated policemen with an unreasonable hatred, and he didn't care very much for Uncle Micah either, because he had never seen anyone quite like him before. David calmed him, and then noticed that the white bow was a twist of chocolate paper. He opened it and saw a note in the twin's best style and headed with a sketch of the Lone Pine. He beckoned Jenny to his side, and they read together.

"To our galant Reskewers.

"We are imprissoned here without much hope. But do not worry about the rope bekos Tom is undoing his pullover and we will let it down for the rope. Peter sends her love to all. Tell Uncle Micah to keep a brave heart as all will be well for him as a brighter day has dawned for him and he can claim his heart's desire. We have solved the greatest mistery of all. Love to Henry or Humphrey whichever it is we forget. Up the Lone Pine from Richard and Mary.

"P.S.—Urgent. We are starving specially Dickie."

"What's all this nonsense about Uncle Micah's brave heart, I wonder?" David whispered to Jenny. "But it's not a bad idea to unravel a pullover . . . I'd better tell the old man that, but I don't think I'll give him the other message . . ."

By the time he had reached the grown-ups, Tom had appeared at the window.

"Now then," he called. "I hope it'll reach, but I've tied

my knife at the end. Fix the end of the rope to the wool and I'll haul it up."

The scheme worked well, and to the end of the thin rope was tied a thicker rope which was soon in Tom's eager hands.

"Can you fix the end securely to something inside, lad?" Uncle Micah called. "Or had you better pass it over the cable wire and we'll make a rope cradle for the little 'uns?"

"I can do better than that, sir. I've found a hook and a pulley. If I can get this rope through the pulley we're O.K. . . . O.K. we are, sir . . . If the cable can carry the car it can take our weight one at a time . . . Here she comes, sir."

Now it was plain sailing and David and Jenny watched in admiration as Humphrey deftly made a cradle out of rope and straps of the haversack and fixed it firmly to the end of the hauling rope. Then it was tested with David in the cradle while Humphrey heaved him up a few feet.

"Can you manage those little 'uns?" Uncle Micah called. "Are you there, Petronella? Can you and that lad get them one at a time into the cradle and push 'em off safe?"

"Yes, we'll manage, Uncle," Peter called. "Trust us; but let's hurry, 'cos it's getting dark."

Up went the cradle and Tom hauled it over the edge, and an excited squeaking betrayed Mary as the first passenger. Down below the policeman and Humphrey took the strain, Tom pushed the cradle gently clear of the cliff from above and down she came.

No sooner was she on the ground than she rushed over to Uncle Micah, seized his hand and led him a little way down the track. The old man seemed to be rather dazed and quite willing to leave the rescue arrangements to someone else. Before the cradle went up again, David noticed that he passed his hand several times across his forehead. Then Mary dragged at his arm, and he lowered his head for her to whisper. No doubt the twins were up to something mysterious, but it must be important, David thought, or else Mary would have waited to see Dickie come down.

Dickie's descent was not without incident, because he was so excited that he swung the cradle until he hit the side of the cliff and hurt himself.

"Mountaineerin'," he said, "that's what this is. Everest! And down there you're the native porters. Hi! Keep me off the cliff, you porters! . . . Ow! You beasts! . . . I bet you told them to do that, David. You never think of Mary and me doin' all this for you and sufferin' hunger and thirst . . . Oh, gosh! Am I down? Isn't it quick? Give me a sandwich, 'cos I'm famishin'."

And with his mouth full he dashed over to join his twin and Uncle Micah. The cradle went up again and Tom hauled it over the edge and called to them to wait for a bit and then disappeared.

David went over to pat Sally and watched the twins. Humphrey and the policeman sat down and lit their pipes and Jenny was talking to Macbeth. Every now and then David could hear the twins evidently pleading with Mr. Sterling. And then Mary raised her voice, and David heard her say:

"But you *must*, Uncle. It's the most wonderful thing in the world, and we've done it for you. We're not playing a game—honest, we're not, Uncle—so do please, *PLEASE*, believe us! Will you PLEASE, please wish for your heart's desire?"

"Just wish for what you want to happen most in all the world," Dickie said grandly. "An' we'll do it for you . . . Just like that . . . Poof!" and he snapped his fingers and waved a magnificent hand as if he was Merlin himself.

"An' if you can't think what *is* your heart's desire," came Mary's anxious treble, "we'll tell you," and then, before David could see how the old man was reacting, Tom called, "Right away," and down came Peter, laughing all over her brown face. She slipped an arm through David's and said:

"Isn't it grand to be together again, David? Listen—

you two men as well—I can't explain how the twins found him, but it's true—Uncle Micah's son, Charles Sterling is in there with a twisted ankle, and he's coming down next."

David whistled, Jenny looked blank, Humphrey sat down suddenly and the policeman mopped his forehead again. Then Peter waved to Dickie, who was grimacing and walking backwards down the track, while Mary kept Uncle Micah's back to them. When he saw Peter's signal he turned and took the old man's other hand. Then they led him to the lonely hawthorn some fifty yards away, and, to everyone's astonishment, blindfolded him with his own handkerchief. And to all this he submitted seemingly without complaint and sat down with his back to the tree. Mary bent and whispered to him, kissed his cheek and then dashed back to the others with her eyes blazing with excitement.

"Go on! Go on! What are you waiting for?" she hissed when she reached them. "Is he up there, Peter darling? Is he safe?"

"He's all right, but it was an awful job getting him up the ladder. I pulled and poor old Tom pushed. But he's there now."

"Right," called Tom from above, and up shot the cradle. "He's heavy. Better have David and Peter on the rope as well."

Then they saw Charles Sterling pushing himself along to the edge of the ledge. He grinned at them and waved his cigarette as he got his bad ankle first through the ropes of the cradle. But Tom was there to help him, and soon he was sinking gently to the ground, where helping hands were waiting.

"Well, Humphrey," he said as if it was only yesterday that he had gone away, "how do?" and he shook hands and then smiled at David and Jenny and said, "Well done, kids, and thanks a lot."

Then Mary took charge.

"Your broken-hearted father is waiting for you over there,

Uncle Charles. I promised you. *We* promised you, I mean, didn't we? I asked him to say his heart's desire and he was too shy to say it was you, but I know you are. Can you get there with a stick? He promised to wait there till someone took the hankie off his eyes. He looks lonely, doesn't he?"

"So do you, Uncle Charles," said Dickie suddenly, as he looked up at him.

The big man laughed shakily. "Maybe I am! Wait here, all of you. I'll manage with this stick," and he hobbled over towards the hawthorn.

"Don't watch them, you beasts!" Mary cried, and turned her back.

"Oh, well," said Dickie, as he found two more sandwiches, "we've done it again. Mary and me can do these things."

"Well, I'd be much obliged if you'd do something for me instead of talking so much," came peevishly from Tom who was still aloft. "What about me?"

So Peter and David, rather ashamed, sent up the cradle and brought their friend down. Peter was loud in praise of Tom's pluck in riding the cable car, and Tom could not say enough for Peter. And when they all looked over to the hawthorn there were Uncle Micah and Uncles Charles shaking hands with each other and talking together and laughing together until Uncle Micah roared suddenly:

"Humphrey, ye great idle, good-for-nothing, don't stand there gaping, but bring the pony for the lad. Can't you see he's come home?"

And so, as the sun slipped down behind the mountain ridge and dark night came rushing up the Dingle and the Chair loomed menacingly over all again, a strange procession wound slowly down the track. First came the large policeman, for it was fitting that he should lead. Then came a well-laden Humphrey leading Sally, on which Charles was riding. By his side strode Uncle Micah, with his head held high. Next, hand in hand, trudged the twins —tired now, but very happy and proud. Next came Macbeth, who was prepared to accept all the inconvenience

and humiliation of a ridiculous procession like this if only
he could get home and find some peace. All these humans
seemed to have gone mad today, and he hoped soon to
forget the awful experience of being put into a large bucket
and rushed through the air. When a rabbit rustled in a
fern in front of him, he proceeded unmoved on his dignified
way.

And after Macbeth came Tom and Jenny. Tom was
swaggering a little because Jenny wanted to hear all his
adventures several times over, and it is difficult not to
repeat yourself when your listener keeps saying: "You
didn't, Tom? Not *really*?"

But David and Peter, behind them, had not much to say.
They were the sort of friends who do not have to talk a lot
to understand each other.

Once an owl drifted silently over their heads as the moon
came up over the mountain and drenched the hillsides in
silver. David looked up at him as he called his mournful
cry.

"Reminds me of Witchend when I hear an owl . . .
It's been a grand day, after all, Peter," was all he said.

12. Seven White Gates

Much to his fury, Dickie slept late the next morning. He dreamt that Uncle Micah, whirling a lassoo round his head and mounted on Sally, was chasing him round the black rocks of the Devil's Chair. The dream became a nightmare when, as he stumbled and fell, the rope caught his ankle. He struggled fiercely, but the grip tightened. He wriggled, twisted, and sat up in his sleeping-bag and rubbed the sleep from his eyes.

A cool breeze came freshly from the open door of the barn and the sunlight was playing among the cobwebby old rafters above his head. The hay in which he was lying smelled very sweet. Uncle Micah had vanished and Mary had taken his place. She was kneeling at his feet and shaking her curls back as she tugged at his ankle.

"What a lazy little boy you are, Dickie. Generally it's me that can't stay awake, but David says you grunted like anything when he called you and you wouldn't move . . . GET UP! We've got lots to do today."

Before he could answer, Peter's clear laugh came over the top of the partition.

"Poor little chap! Of course he's exhausted. Let him sleep the day through, David . . . I've eaten his breakfast, anyway."

Dickie jumped up with a cry of anguish and struggled out of his sleeping-bag.

"What a lot of beasts you are!" he yelled. "Gimme my breakfast." He hauled up his pyjama trousers, which were coming off with the sleeping-bag, and strode with dignity over to the stove, where Peter was sitting back on her heels trying to toast an old crust.

"This is for the little boy, David," she was saying. "And we'll leave a message with Aunt Carol to look in later and bring him a hot-water bottle . . ."

"And she'd better take his temperature, too," David added. "But we must get along . . . Funny how Mary's growing up more quickly than little Richard, isn't it?"

"Why, look, David! Here is the little chap! Do you think he's walking in his sleep?"

"Where's my breakfast, you beastly beasts?" demanded Dickie, running his fingers through his tousled hair.

So they had mercy on him, and Peter produced a plate of tepid sausages and a boiled egg as well. Mary brought a rug and he sat close against the stove and made up for lost time, while David told him what had happened after they got back to Seven Gates the night before, because neither of the twins remembered much except mugs of hot soup before being carried to their respective beds.

"Those cowboy friends of yours must have told somebody about Uncle Charles and about this place, 'cos in the middle of all the excitement . . ."

"And was there some excitement?" Peter broke in. "Of course, you kids were asleep in your little bags by then, but Uncle Micah was so excited that Aunt Carol didn't know what to say or do next, and they both fussed round Uncle Charles, who was pushed into a comfy chair with his bad foot up on another, and we all felt in the way . . ."

"What happened to Jenny?" asked Dickie with his mouth full. "I like red-headed girls. They're jolly rare."

"She went home with that comic policeman," David explained. "Tom has gone down now to fetch her, and we hope the bobby told that old stepmother of hers not to bully her. Anyway, we were all just coming across the yard when one of those Yankee jeeps came up through the wood and your two pals——"

"Pards," said Dickie. "Pards we call each other. Not pals. Pals is sissy."

"All right," David continued. "Pards, then. They'd

come for Uncle Charles, and he went back with them."

"Is he coming back to see us?"

"They said something about coming back this afternoon, and if Uncle Charles is stationed near here, I s'pose we'll see him again."

Dickie put his fork down with a dramatic gesture.

"An' can't you think of anything better than that? Is that all you can organize while I bin restin'? Tell you what . . . You're none of you any good without me . . . an' Mary's not much good either," he added darkly.

Dumbfounded by this impertinence, David and Peter looked at each other in silence. Then Mary laughed.

"I know what he's going to say," she shouted. "It's the best idea ever. Trust us to think of plans. I know, Dickie. You tell them. It's a reunion."

Dickie passed his empty plate with a lordly air to Peter —who took it without a word—and fumbled for a handkerchief to wipe his mouth.

"All right," he said when he had used the edge of the blanket instead, "I'll tell you. What we want is a whopping, wizard, slap-up reunion feast all done by us in here. When something good has happened it's always good to do some feastin'," and he looked round complacently.

David laughed.

"You win, Dickie. Trust you to think of eating— 'specially when your mouth is full already. It's a grand idea."

"That's O.K., pards," said Dickie, rising languidly from his stool and stretching.

"Just let us know when you want some ideas," added Mary.

"We'll want something extra special for this feast. A bit of old corn beef is no good," Dickie said, as he wandered over towards his clothes.

"Venzun, maybe," suggested Mary.

"You're all so DULL today, it's just frightenin'," Dickie continued. "Uncle Charles is the prodigal son, isn't he? Jus' go and ask old Uncle Beaver to kill the fatted calf.

He'll do it for us—me, I mean. You jus' ask him," and he disappeared triumphantly into his cubicle.

Then Peter went in to find Aunt Carol and told her of the big plan and invited her and Uncle Micah to be the Lone Piners' guests that evening. As a result of this interview, Humphrey—in a rare state of excitement this morning—was sent to kill the two fattest geese on the farm, and Aunt Carol was very apologetic because they hadn't got any venison.

"You can't cook two geese on that stove, my dear, so you'd better use this kitchen as much as you like . . . And how are you going to let Charles and those other men know about the feast? Charles said he was coming over this afternoon, but if you want them all you'd better ride over now and ask them. I can tell you how to get to their headquarters—Charles told me—it's only about six miles away . . . Your uncle thinks that there's nobody like David just at present—after his Charles, of course—so he'd better go and find him and tell him your plans."

So Peter rode off on Sally and David went to find Uncle Micah, while Dickie and Mary sat on the white gate at the top of the wood and gloated over their adventure of yesterday and the feast to come. After a little, Tom and Jenny came up the track, but were not much impressed by the twins' air of mystery, as they had met Peter on the way, who had told them of the new plans. Then Mrs. Sterling came out and set them all to work cleaning and preparing the barn, and Uncle Micah came striding in from the fields with David panting at his heels. Henry was summoned from some mysterious haunt at the back of the cowsheds and sent to fetch a big trestle table and benches from one of the lofts.

"Pity we can't give 'em a concert," Dickie said to Mary. "Like we used to do at home at Christmas."

"I might recite," Mary said modestly. "I'm pretty good. Or we might sing a carol, twin!"

But before they could decide what to do unselfishly for the entertainment of the others, Mrs. Sterling bustled up and sent them into the garden for some cabbages. When they got back, and just as Dickie was feeling hungry again, Peter rode into the farmyard with the news that Uncle Charles, Jerry, Jake and a friend would be coming about four o'clock.

"This friend of theirs is fun," she said as she slipped off Sally's back. "He's a real cowboy, Dickie. At least Jerry said he was, and they all winked at me and the new one called me 'Sister.' . . Hello, Tom. Hello, Jenny! Where's David? . . . Golly! Doesn't the barn look grand? Let's decorate it with evergreens."

Aunt Carol had found time to cut sandwiches for lunch. While they ate and worked Uncle Micah crossed the yard once or twice and Mary said she heard him whistling.

"That's nothing," Jenny announced. "He *waved* to me once."

The others looked at her in astonishment.

"Are you sure he wasn't chasing away some old fly or something?" Dickie asked.

Jenny shook her head.

"No. He waved to me . . . all friendly . . . I think he's nice, and I'm going to tell everybody in Barton 'bout him. I don't think he's a wizard any more. The spell's been lifted."

David, who was standing on a wobbly chair on the top of the trestle-table trying to tie a branch of feathery larch to one of the rafters, looked down and said:

"I meant to ask you before, Jenny. Have you run away again? What did Mrs. Harman say when Tom came?"

"Don't you worry about that," Tom answered. "Jenny's one of us now, and Mrs. Sterling gave me a proper invite for her. The old woman pretended she was glad Jenny was asked, but I dunno what'll happen if there's a run on stamps this afternoon, as Jen's not there to help."

David looked surprised and dropped the hammer.

"That's grand, Jenny," he said. "And I'm glad, but I thought it was rather a rag when you kept running away."

"Close the castle doors," Dickie shouted suddenly. "Let down the drawbridge, 'cos it's going to rain!"

"It's raining," Mary confirmed. "Quickly! The table's getting wet this end."

So they closed the big doors, as a fierce storm swept up over the pinewood and sent old Humphrey scurrying for shelter.

"It's dark with the doors closed, and I expect it will be dark for the feast," Jenny said. "Can't we find some lanterns? That paper sort that used to catch on fire would be fun."

When Mrs. Sterling was asked if she had any such treasures she stopped rolling her pastry long enough to put a dab of flour on Jenny's freckled nose and say, "Try the attic. There's any amount of rubbish up there."

After ten minutes' hectic exploration with Tom, they found ten splendid specimens which David helped them to hang with wire to the rafters of the barn. They closed the doors again, and tried out the effect by lighting the candles in each, and at once the old barn glowed with colour.

But the twins soon got bored with the display and climbed up to the loft, where they sat on Peter's mattress and watched another rain-storm whipping the puddles in the yard into a fury and turning the cart-ruts into miniature torrents. Mary was the first to hear the lorry coming up the track, but it was Dickie who saw Jake jump out to open the last white gate. By the time the lorry had pulled up in the yard, the twins had dashed down and flung back the white doors of the barn.

"Hyar there, pards!" Dickie called. "Howdy, folks!"

Then the head of Jerry and a stranger poked out from the canvas covering of the lorry, while Uncle Charles opened the door at the front and called:

"Hello, kids! Had your sleep out? We've come to your party."

Jake helped him down and he limped over to the house, remarking that he would see them later, while the twins made a great business of introducing the other Lone Piners.

"These are our friends from America," Dickie explained.
"This one is Jerry, and this one is Jake, and this one . . .
what's your name, pard?" he hissed to the stranger . . .
"this one is Larry, and I think, chaps . . . I *think* he's a
cowboy."

Then followed a wonderful half-hour, for their new
friends had brought plenty of exciting food for the feast,
and a concertina. Larry really was a cowboy, and when
Tom found him a rope he did the most amazing tricks with
a lasso. Jake was the artist with the concertina, and while
Peter was busy at the stove he sat on the stairs just above
her and sang her songs from Dixie and Alabama. Then
Aunt Carol brought the news that the geese would be ready
in ten minutes, and would Peter and Jenny help her dish up
while the others sat down and kept out of the way?

Fortunately, the lorry had brought plenty of drinks,
including a dozen bottles of Coca Cola, and these kept
Dickie busy, while David arranged the positions at table.
He put Uncle Micah at the top, with Charles on his right
and Peter on his left. Mary was next to Charles, and, of
course, Dickie next his twin, then Larry and Jake. At the
opposite side of the table David didn't see why he shouldn't
be next to Peter, and then came Jenny, Tom and Jerry.
Mrs. Sterling was to be at the other end opposite her
husband.

"Table's too long really," David said. "But it's all we
could get. We want some more people to fill it . . . Has
anyone seen Uncle Micah, by the way?"

But only Charles answered. "I have. He'll be along soon,
I guess, but if he's not here when the food comes—and
here it is—I'll carve."

Flushed but triumphant, Aunt Carol then entered with
the sizzling dishes while the girls followed with trays of
vegetables. Another violent storm had come up, so Dickie
had to close the doors as soon as they were in.

Jenny looked up proudly at the coloured lanterns
glowing over their heads.

"More like Christmas," she said. "Golly! doesn't that goose smell lovely?" She turned to Tom. "D'you know," she whispered, "that I used to be scared of this place and old Uncle Micah, but I'm not now. I wonder where he is?"

Mary was leaning across her twin to ask Larry what he did with the wild cows when he caught them, when Jake drawled:

"Say, folks, who's the stranger?"

Standing just over the threshold with the doors half closed behind him was a tall man in an old-fashioned dark suit. He stood awkwardly and a little shyly fingering his chin. His eyes were dark and piercing and reminded David of somebody.

Everyone stopped talking and stared. Aunt Carol looked up at the stranger and smiled. Mary was the only one to see this quick look, and suddenly she jumped on to the bench, flung back her curls, and shouted:

"Don't you see who it is, you sillies? It's Uncle Micah with his beard off!"

"Gosh!" Dickie whispered, "we're right again, twin. He's been disguised all the time. Now he's not Uncle Beaver any more."

There was an awkward silence until Mr. Sterling laughed a little nervously and called to Aunt Carol.

"Do you recognise your husband, Caroline? . . . It feels mighty strange and cold without it." Then he looked down the long table until his eyes rested on Mary, still standing, flushed and excited, on the bench. He beckoned to her. "I have something for you, my child."

Mary jumped to the floor and walked over to him. She stood with her hands behind her back, while the light from the lanterns above the table glowed on her curls, and looked up at him fearlessly. She had never been frightened of him. There was a pause while Dickie strolled over to her side, and then Mr. Sterling stooped and lifted her until she was standing on the table. Then he addressed the company.

"Yesterday this child brought me my heart's desire. Tell me now, Mary, what is *your* heart's desire?"

She looked puzzled for a moment and glanced down at Dickie and then round at all the faces staring at her. Then she announced promptly:

"For Mummy to be here—and Daddy, too, home from the war to have fun with us here."

Uncle Micah threw back his head and laughed a great laugh. "I knew it! . . . Richard, open the doors."

And almost before Dickie had pushed them right back, Mary had jumped from the table, dashed out of the barn and flung herself at a tall man in Air Force uniform who was standing smiling in the drizzle. Then David ran out, too. Both his father and mother were there, and Peter followed him as she saw her own Daddy standing quietly in the background.

Then there was pandemonium as places were found for the new-comers at the feast and as more plates were fetched. Mrs. Morton found time to give Peter a hug and Tom a smile and a handshake before introducing them to her husband. Then the twins dragged her over to the rather shy and bewildered Jenny so that she didn't feel left out, while Peter's father continued to shake the hand of his nephew Charles.

"This is a great day," he was heard to say. "A great day, Charles, my boy. Many a time I've told your father that you'd be back one day, and it's strange to me that you should come in this way from foreign parts . . . And you've seen my little Petronella? A good girl, she is . . . a little wild and headstrong and not too fond of her studies, but she'll settle down . . . Ah, well! God bless you, my boy. . . . Your father's a changed man already . . ."

But not until everybody had met everyone else and nobody felt a stranger would Mrs. Morton explain how they had arrived precisely in time to fulfil Mary's heart's desire.

"It's easy really. Daddy wired suddenly yesterday that he was coming home for ten days today and I went this afternoon to meet him at Onnybrook. On the platform he asked where you all were, and while I was explaining, Mr. Sterling, who was on the same train, joined us. While we were talking, Dr. Mansfield drove up and spoke to Daddy and said he had been called to Barton and would we like a lift to come and see you. And here we are! We walked up together through the wood and met Mr. Micah Sterling in the yard, who asked us to wait so that we could give you a surprise. The Doctor's calling for us again later tonight, but we want you all to come home tomorrow now Daddy's here."

Dickie was then heard to say:

"Of couse we're very pleased to see you, Daddy, and we've got a lot of adventures to tell you, We practically died of starvation in that old mine, an' if it hadn't been for my pards here I 'spect our skeletons would be whitenin' in the sun."

"Only there wasn't any sun in there," Mary broke in. "Just awful gloom and dripping walls!"

Then a great chattering broke out again, so that it was difficult for the children to find anyone to answer the hundreds of questions that had to be asked. The Americans were friendly to everyone, but not very interested in an old farmhouse with seven gates and a master who used to stride the hills at night. Dickie, of course, could never tire of hearing his pards tell him stories of their own land, but it was a chance remark of Jake's that answered Jenny's biggest worry.

"Waal," he drawled, "reckon we've all got to know this funny lil' country o' yours purty well these last few months. . . . We done purty well everything round here day and night."

Peter heard the last sentence and leaned forward and shouted:

"What do you mean, Jake? Day and night?"

"Waal, we bin most everywhere. We bin up them blamed rocks—on hands and knees by ourselves and then in hundreds. We bin on top o' the little hill way over there that you call a mountain on hosses and in tanks and in trucks. Many a time, too, we bin *inside* the hill, and one day Jerry and me and Sergeant Bill—but you ain't met him yet—come over the lil' valley one misty evenin' in that quaint lil' ole car on wires . . . Shore thing! We done 'bout everything round here, haven't we, pards?"

Jenny's hands were white as she gripped the table. Her eyes were wide as she gasped, "The Black Riders! You were the Riders!"

Peter's laugh rang out, "And it was the American Army went over our heads that night, Jenny! D'you remember?"

In the pause that followed, Dickie's voice sounded loud and clear.

"Gosh, twin! We seen 'em too. That night . . . High on top we saw them."

Now Peter was crazy to ask whether there really *was* a mystery about Seven Gates and why there had to be seven gates and why Charles ran away and whether this barn was anything to do with him in the old days; but although Uncle Micah seemed to be a changed man, she didn't feel she could really ask anybody. And then, just as if she knew what she was thinking, Aunt Carol called from the end of the table:

"Come and help me with the coffee, Peter. No, thanks, Jenny. Peter and I can manage."

Outside the air was fresh and clear after the stuffy barn, and Peter stood for a minute and breathed deeply. Her head was aching with the excitement and the tobacco smoke of the grown-ups, and she suddenly felt a fierce longing for the hills of home. She never had enjoyed crowds, anyway, and with a sudden pang she realized that she had hardly spoken to her own father. She sighed. "Lovely to go home tomorrow," she was thinking, when Aunt Carol called softly across the yard:

"Come along in, Peter dear. I want to talk to you while the coffee is getting hot."

Ten minutes later when they came back across the yard,

Peter looked very serious. She held open the door for her aunt and said: "Ask David to come out, please, Auntie. I must tell him but I promise I won't tell anybody else."

And when a bewildered David slipped out into the moonlight, Peter had her back to him and was leaning on the white gate leading down to the wood.

"What's up, Peter? I say, isn't it a rag the parents turning up. What a grand night."

"Let's walk down through the wood, David. We won't be long and I want some fresh air. I've got something to tell you . . . It's about Uncle Micah," she began as they stepped into the dark shadows of the trees. "Aunt Carol's just told me 'cos she was sure we were curious and afraid we might ask . . . I was just going to, matter of fact, when she called me over to the house! I'll tell you quickly, and she says if we know we needn't really tell anyone else.

"She says that Uncle Micah has always been queer and that he once told her that he took this farm because of a dream. He did a lot of preaching I b'lieve before he was married and he came here because he once dreamed of a farm with seven white gates. He found this place in an awful mess, but there were only six gates, and it was Aunt Martha who came to see it with him, and persuaded him to take it. It was cheap because nobody else could make it pay, I s'pose. When he said he must follow his dream because the Lord had sent it—that's what Aunt Carol says—Aunt Martha, who must have been rather a darling, said she'd make seven gates by painting the barn door white. An' so she did, an' after, when things went badly, Uncle Micah said the place was cursed and when Aunt Martha died he was sure. Auntie didn't say much about Charles— p'raps she doesn't know—but I guess that Uncle Micah was unkind to him and they quarrelled, and that's why he ran away."

"Golly!" said David. "Poor old man! What a miserable time he must have had."

"And what about Aunt Carol and Aunt Martha?" Peter asked indignantly. "They must have had the rotten time . . . Anyway, after Charles went it seems Uncle really was queer. He worked here like mad and made it pay at last, but only Henry and Humphrey would stay with him and stories were told about him in Barton 'cos he wandered about the Stiperstones at night. For years and years Aunt Carol says there were nights when he never slept at all, and used to walk and walk up the Dingle and over the Chair till everyone was scared of him and even children ran away from him—that's why he was so different when Mary wasn't afraid of him. An' he's never stopped grieving for Charles—never *once*, Auntie says. Worse and worse he got till he forgot to speak like ordinary people . . . and Aunt Carol didn't say anything about what she'd done to help him, but when she told me that he'd slept all last night through, she cried, David—and so did I a bit, too."

There was silence for a minute while David unlatched the gate leading into the lane.

Then he said: "Mary says that they followed him up the Dingle and lost him because Mackie ran after a rabbit. I s'pose when he heard us talking about the twins with Mrs. Sterling in the barn next morning, he was afraid they might have followed him, and that's why he looked so awful."

Peter nodded. "I s'pose so. Perhaps he felt guilty about them, and yet wasn't sure if he'd done anything or not. You know how beastly you feel sometimes when you can't quite remember. Anyway, Aunt Carol says it's all a miracle, and Uncle says the curse is lifted at last and that we've all lifted it. An' he's cut his beard off and he's talking to Daddy as if he was a real person and not a congregation, and we've had another good adventure."

David didn't answer. He was standing with one hand on the gate listening. Peter stood still, too.

"Can you hear it, Peter? It's a man singing!"

"And wheels, too! David! It couldn't be, could it? Wait a bit and I'll prove it."

She fumbled at her neck and pulled up the little carved wood whistle which Fenella had given her in Barton a few days ago. When the faint voice stopped, she put the whistle to her lips and blew with all her breath. The wheels stopped then, and she sounded the sweet, piercing call again. This time an answering whistle came at once, and the horse's hooves were heard again as he was urged into a trot.

Peter grabbed David's hand. "It's true, David! It's true! They said the Romanies would answer that whistle, and they have. It may be Reuben! Come on! Let's go and meet them," and together they raced down the moonlit lane till the dear, familiar, coloured caravan breasted the hill with Reuben himself at the piebald's head.

"It's all right, Reuben," Peter called. "Don't hurry. It's only us, and I blew the whistle to see if you'd answer."

Miranda was on the driving seat and her teeth flashed as she saw them both standing hand in hand in the moonlight. She threw back her head and laughed and said, "Shall I tell the future for you tonight, my pretty one?" and Peter felt a little foolish as she shook her head and snatched her hand away from David's.

But Reuben was not so pleased because the horse was blowing and he was out of breath himself.

"The whistle is only for danger," he said as he wiped his forehead. "Is there no danger?"

Then Peter explained and David told how they had found their way over the mountain, and Reuben said that they had come a little way out of their journey back into Wales to see if all was well with them and that one of them would have braved the road to Seven Gates in the morning.

"Best wait till the morning. Camp just here," Peter pleaded, "and we'll all come and see you again. We're going home tomorrow, but David and I must get back now else they'll think we've started walking in our sleep."

So the caravan pulled in to the grass verge at the side of the road, and they called "Good night" and "See you in the morning," and ran up through the whispering wood again.

The yard was bright in the moonlight and from the barn came a confused murmur of talk and singing and music from the concertina and the clink of china. They looked up at the Devil's Chair, gleaming sharp and black against the star-spangled sky, and Peter slipped her arm through David's as he stood with his hands in his pockets.

"The spell is broken I'm sure, David. I s'pose it's like most bad things—they're never so real when you're not afraid of them. Anyway, I bet old Seven Gates' curse has gone for ever . . . Let's open the doors a bit and peep at them."

The coloured lanterns still glowed mistily through the blue smoke. The Americans were making Aunt Carol laugh but Larry had Dickie sitting on the table in front of him showing him how to tie knots in a rope. Tom and Jenny were singing to the concertina and, at the other end of the table, Mr. Morton, the two Mr. Sterlings and Charles were talking together in a cloud of smoke. Mary was asleep on her father's shoulder, and her mother was supporting her on the other side.

Mrs. Morton felt the current of air through the open door and was the first to look up and smile as she saw David and Peter.

Peter tightened her hold on her friend's arm.

"David," she whispered. "I've got an idea. Tell them we'll be back in an hour or see them tomorrow if they've gone before we're back. Let's borrow old Uncle Micah's cob—he wouldn't mind for once—and I'll get Sally and let's ride up the Dingle together in the moonlight, like Wild Edric and Godda."

"What about the others?" David grinned.

"No. There aren't enough horses. We'll do it on our own. Tell your mother now."

So David slipped across to Mrs. Morton and whispered,

and after a pause she nodded. Then he was outside again with Peter.

As they pushed the big white doors together and ran across the yard, they heard one of the twins say:

"There you are again, you two beasts . . . You're plannin' things without us. Wait! We're coming too."